INTIMATE EVIL

INTIMATE EVIL

a novel by
PAUL REIDINGER

DONALD I. FINE, INC.
NEW YORK

Library of Congress Cataloging-in-Publication Data

Reidinger, Paul.
Intimate evil: a novel / by Paul Reidinger.
p. cm.
ISBN: 1-55611-140-1
I. Title.
PS3568.E479I56   1989
813'.54—dc19   88-46165

Manufactured in the United States of America
10   9   8   7   6   5   4   3   2   1

Designed by Irving Perkins Associates

for N.

PART I
TRIALS

1

Dawn. Night sky leaking salmon. Down the bars, the sweating concrete blocks, onto the face. Puffy, overstuffed clouds. Rain on the way. The dusty shafts of morning light play funny games: the nose seems longer; so do the lashes; the whiskers heavier and darker. He hasn't shaved in several days.

Cocks crowing in barnyards some miles distant. The scent of hay and corn, pigs and summer. Farmers milking the cows, firing up the combines. Rumblings of thunder. Out there. Not here.

He opens his eyes and wonders for a moment—though he has been here, in this very spot, for more than a year— where he is. He starts, remembers. His neck is stiff from having slept with his head jammed against the wall for most of the night. A quiet night. No visits. No departures. No midnight announcement.

A faint smell of shit in the air. Also chlorine.

The cells, including his cell, are about 100 yards

away—down to the end of the row, through a set of heavy steel doors, down a corridor dimly lit by bare bulbs, into a small chamber—no more than ten feet square—painted a sickly green, the color of Comet.

One of Jason's neighbors on the cell block made his brother-in-law eat Comet. Then he shot him twice in the right ear. Brains and blood all over the flowered wallpaper in the kitchen.

It is said to take about two minutes, more or less, to get there. But of course that's the direct route, not the scenic. It takes about two minutes, more or less, to do it.

Along one wall of the green chamber is a long Plexiglass shield behind which the witnesses sit, four across, three deep. Twelve witnesses in all, as required by state law. Black drapes divide them from the scene: opened briefly, closed. Like a play. The tiled floor slopes downward to a drain. Just in case.

There is a black telephone on the wall near the door, where the warden stands. Just in case.

Behind the chair itself is another window; the operator stands there, cloaked in black, like a villain from a medieval tale. Dials, buttons, a big toggle switch: the trappings of modernity, the humane advancement of science. First used a century ago.

The chair itself is made of oak, but the straps are leather. Built by the inmates themselves in 1931, from trees grown on prison property. Grisly Gretchen, they call her. He has never seen Grisly Gretchen. But he has dreamed about her.

The cells themselves, twenty of them, are lined up like cells in a honeycomb. They are all the same size, all painted the same off-white color, all equipped the same way: bed, toilet, wash basin. There aren't enough of them, though, so not everyone with a date with Gretchen is waiting so near her. A group of them are somewhere else in the prison, not quite so close to the green chamber. No one has ever seen them.

It's Tuesday: shower day. The guard comes by at a quarter to seven, rattles the keys in the lock. Another guard stands behind, watching.

"Let's go, kid," the guard says gruffly.

He extends his hands and the guard puts on the handcuffs. He does this deftly, gently. The other guard watches, hand resting on holster. Off they go to the shower, the prisoner loping along in the middle, the two guards to either side and slightly behind. He knows where to go, and the guards talk quietly to each other about baseball. Not much different from walking a dog. A lovely Sunday stroll. Like a family.

The days are not unpleasant, just numbingly the same. His mother was allowed to send him a small black-and-white TV—a gift to commemorate the first Christmas he had ever spent away from his family—but he has taken to reading. Odd that a boy who was always lackadaisical about school should end up taking such an interest in reading. Or in chess—but that's because of Bryan, of course, always the intellectual.

Two weeks from tomorrow is Patrick's twentieth birthday. Jason dreams about him, too: where he is, what he's doing, what he thinks about or feels. You know so little for sure in a place like this, where the tiniest bits of information about the outside world, outside people, are like scraps of food thrown to starving people. Your imagination can get carried away.

And, of course, his father.

Little Colleen is already eleven, already a big help to her mother in the kitchen. For a while they mailed him cookies they'd baked, and the guards X-rayed them to make sure the McGuires hadn't put in a gun or razor blades instead of chocolate chips. But there haven't been cookies in a long time. He hasn't seen his mother, heard from her, in a long time. Nor from Colleen.

He savors the shower, soaping himself down slowly, thoroughly. Every part of his body receives intense attention, and at length he is so lathered up that he looks like a mummy. He is not at all self-conscious of the guards, the fact that their eyes are on him at all times. No privacy, here or anywhere else.

They watch but do not seem to see. Sometimes he plays with himself a little, tries to get a rise out of them, but if they notice they don't show it. The routine is to stand there puffing cigarettes, maybe humming, checking the watch from time to time. He gets five minutes under the hot water.

This morning it has swelled up more than usual, and as he towels himself off one of the guards nods and says, "Not bad for eighteen."

"Yeah."

He buffs dry his mop of auburn hair. He is very conscious of his hair, keeps it short and neat, the sideburns carefully shaved off at the top of the ear, the neck kept clear of undergrowth. Conscious of the fact that the hair will be shaved just before they strap him in. He runs his hand through it to give it that final touch, then slips back into his underwear and pale blue prison fatigues. They take him back to his cell.

Breakfast at eight. Orange juice, farina, sausage links, toast. Coffee if he wants it, but he's not keen on the taste.

Exercise later, in the yard.

And his lawyer is coming.

*   *   *

Monroe is a strikingly beautiful city—all trees and parks and unexpected vistas of the three large lakes that attracted the first settlers. Everything here is prototypically efficient: the buses are all new and make no noise; the mayor is young, good-looking, well-spoken, and has been on the "Today" show; people throw their trash into trash barrels instead of the gutter. Even the graffiti are literate: quotes from Goethe and Schiller, Plato and Bacon (most of this, true, near the university).

From my eighth-floor office I look northwest, across the white marble capitol dome in the middle of its well-trimmed park, toward the largest of the lakes. The water is ringed with bluffs, and in the fall I sometimes sit for a long time just looking at the folds of color.

The governor sits under that dome, as do the state senate and legislature and a host of political aides. Also the Court of Criminal Appeals. Five judges hearing everything from capital appeals to drunk-driving cases. I see them around town from time to time, out with their spouses or addressing the State Bar Association: four middle-aged white men with gray temples. One middle-aged white woman who dyes her hair. They know who I am after a dozen or so arguments before them, although the most I've ever said to any of them, outside the courtroom, is "Hello, Judge," and the most I've ever heard back is "Hello, Counsel." Who says that law school creates sociopaths?

Today the lake reflects the slate sky, and little drops of rain scurry down my window. It's cool for June, though all the rain has made the green things grow wildly.

I find that my hands are shaking as I look through the sentencing report, the order, the automatic stay pending review in the Court of Criminal Appeals, a draft of my brief. It's the caffeine. It's because I'm nervous. I have never been there before, never seen him before, don't really know what to expect.

What will I say?

Columbia State Prison is about two hours north of here, out amid the cornfields and cows. Out among the people who favor the death penalty (but who, overwhelmingly, resisted the prison's being located anywhere near them). It's an easy enough drive—freeway most of the way. Even the rain won't make much difference; I'll get there just after lunch. If I have lunch. The doughnuts Maggie brought in earlier are lying there in my gut like concrete.

The Monroe *Zeitgeist* is liberal—not altogether surprising when you consider this is a university town and the state capital and even the bus drivers have graduate degrees in English. Still, the city is completely misplaced in this rural, conservative state—like a shard of some coastal metropolis that landed here by accident. Monroe is so unlike the rest of Columbia that it has often seemed like a joke to me that it's the state capital. God knows the outstaters regard the city with deep suspicion: it is tolerant of blacks, Cubans, homosexuals; its representatives are always getting up in the state legislature to argue that the state should be "nuke-free," or to demand that America's military conspiracy in Central America be ended or that cars be banned downtown, or to urge that the state's capital-punishment law be repealed. They have had some success, at least locally; it is unlawful to detonate a thermonuclear device within the city limits, and anyone who does so can be punished by a $500 fine. Hotshot physics and engineering undergraduates, beware.

We Delafields have been part of the local scene for most of this century. My father's family were minor English landlords who left the homeland for uncertain reasons sometime late in the last century. My grandfather was born here and grew up to be not only a lawyer but mayor of the city. There is a bronze bust of him, looking rather like Freud, in the lobby of City Hall.

My father, shrewder than I, elected not to challenge the old man on his home field; he became an ophthalmologist and retired at age 60 to a country village across the lake. He and my mother still come in for the occasional play or visit with Jessie, but they have taken to the life of country gentility with great delight. Reverting to family form.

Families are cyclical, I guess; at any rate I followed Grandfather's lead and became a lawyer. Liked the policy questions of Con Law, the majesty of it; now my specialty is appellate litigation. The theories and models are like art, in a way, and bring what I imagine is the same sort of pleasure. The orderliness of appellate argument: no witnesses to clutter things up or make hearsay statements or put jurors off with their shifty eyes; none of that. The pleasure of creating something, of guiding a life. The law is alive, after all. Terrifying thought.

Before I want to law school I thought the death penalty was wrong. The state's taking of life is immoral and all the rest. As heinous as the act of the most vile murderer. How can we as a civilized society etc. Aren't we bigger than that after all these centuries?

But you read a few fact situations in your Crim Law class about what people do to each other and you begin to wonder. Read, for example, about the man who thought his wife was having an affair with the man next door, took his elephant gun to a second-floor bedroom, and mowed down both families. He pleaded "inadequate personality" as a defense and got a four-year sentence.

Read about the three big-city teenagers who didn't have enough money for bus fare. They stopped a medical student on the way home from a night of study, robbed her, beat her to death with a brick, then raped her repeatedly. Total yield: $5.67. More than enough bus fare.

Read enough cases like that—there are hundreds of them, thousands, maybe—and you begin to understand that there are things happening out there for which a prison sentence seems inadequate. Beside the point even. At least that's the way it seems to me. We have to respond; we have to protect ourselves from these people.

In Monroe the issue is one of human rights and sociology and a certain mob mentality. *It's not their fault. It's not the way we should behave, even if they are beasts.* It's not politically correct to suggest otherwise. So I am out of step, though I try not to let it show. I don't want to be an outcast, after all.

So why am I doing this crazy thing? Why am I trying to save this crazy boy who wasted half his family?

It's easy not to think when you drive through the country—easy just to let the countryside unfold like a silent movie. I like to drive this way, totally relaxed, letting some half-conscious part of me guide the Audi through the road's gentle curves, letting the frustrations of practice, office, home, slip away.

Except that they aren't today. For one thing it's begun to rain and the roads are slicking up.

"Be careful," Maggie said. "Do you have your macintosh?"

Maggie's own boys have grown up and gone off to college, so there's no one around the house for her to mother. She comes into the office laden with maternal instinct and slathers it on me like whipped cream in between bouts of typing my correspondence and bringing me doughnuts. She always asks how Caroline is, and little Jessie. Fine, I always say. They are always fine.

"Yes, I do," I said.

"And don't forget to eat something before you get there," she said. "You'll need your strength."

"Don't worry," I said.

"And drive carefully."

I am driving carefully, watching my speed, taking care not to get too close to the car in front of me. The truth is that I haven't been this nervous since moot court. I have never met one of my pro bono clients before. And the truth is that I'm wondering, as the rain comes down and I see the sign that says "Warrensville—Columbia State Prison 16," why I have abandoned that comfortable impersonality.

Three days a week Jason works out in the rancid little weight room. His exercise time is limited, so he has learned to go through his routine with some efficiency. Bench press, biceps, triceps, delts; then to the leg machine for thighs and calves; repeat the routine twice. It takes him about a half an hour to complete his three sets. Sit-ups if he has time; otherwise he does them in his cell.

"Let's go, kid," one of the guards says, and he is led out into the yard. The sky is gray and damp but the showers have paused for a while. He does his calesthenics: jumping jacks, knee bends, push-ups; afterward he runs in place for ten minutes. There is nowhere to run. The yard is enclosed by razor-sharp barbed wire, and some yards beyond guards sit in watchtowers, rifles at the ready.

Jason is in terrific shape, better shape than he's ever been in his life. He is pleased at all the muscles he sees when he looks at himself naked in the mirror after a shower,

pleased by the cords in his arms, the formidable bulge of
his pecs, his legs long and solid. He feels good. He feels as if
he's making progress, that he's not the same kid he was
sixteen months ago.

After breakfast he wrote his mother a letter:

Dear Ma,

It's raining today. It woke me up this morning, and
then there was some thunder. No lightning, though. Did
it rain there?

My lawyer is coming today. He lives in Monroe. He
heard somehow that I needed a lawyer. I can't pay him,
though. He wrote me a letter saying I was not to worry
about things.

Ma, I know you're worried about me but don't be. I just
got this feeling that everything is going to be fine. I think
about you and Colleen often and I hope you are well. I am
very well.

Your son,
Jason

P.S. Please send more cookies.

He put it in an envelope and addressed it to the family's old
home in Batavia. Perhaps it would be forwarded. Perhaps
one day she would start writing to him again.

As he finishes his last set of squat-thrusts it begins to
sprinkle again, drippings from a gray shroud that hides
the distant hills and reduces the watchtowers to ghostly
shadows. He jogs back toward the cell block, and the
guards reattach his handcuffs for the brief walk to his cell.
He will wait there for a half hour or so until lunch is ready.
It will come to him, overcooked and pooled in grease, on a
tray. In the meantime he will page through a book his new
lawyer has sent him. It's a play by Shakespeare. *Romeo and
Juliet.* It looks hard but he will give it a try.

*   *   *

The reason is this: our system is adversarial, and therefore it depends on both sides arguing as forcefully, as effectively as possible in order to work properly. You're a fool to walk into court without a lawyer, because the other side sure as hell will have one, and they'll eat you alive.

Lawyers cost money, of course, and money is not something eighteen-year-old boys on death row have a lot of. Our firm, Petit & Tuttle, is famous for its sense of public commitment and its role in Democratic politics in this city and state (in the city there's barely any other kind). Both the founding partners were governors, in successive terms. When I explained to them that I might be interested in doing some pro bono work for death-row inmates, they were both instantly supportive.

You know, of course, they said, that the full resources of the firm are at your disposal. Associates, if you need them. Don't worry about the time. We will work everything out.

I'm doing this so the system works the way it's supposed to. So justice is done. That's what I told the senior partners, and that's what I told the Court of Criminal Appeals. I'm willing to represent one or two of these guys, I said, but please not the absolute dogs I don't want saved any more than you do. Give me somebody I can deal with.

I think we've got just the thing for you, the clerk of court said, as though he were about to show me a tie for my new suit. He's a juvenile, just turned eighteen. Multiple homicide. Family killing. Pretty grisly stuff, but there were mitigating circumstances that weren't brought out at trial. Could have a pretty strong inadequate-representation case, the clerk added helpfully.

My breath caught slightly when he said "juvenile"—

we are sentencing children to death?—but I believe that some "children" deserve all the punishment we can give them. Some children aren't children at all, just murderous, evil people who happen to be seventeen or sixteen or even fifteen or fourteen or younger. Who understand how reluctant the system is to deal them a real blow.

But something about this boy's case told me that he's not really a bad kid, that something really crazy drove him over the edge. He just doesn't look the way a murderer ought to look: he looks like an angel, with those small Irish features and that Irish hair. He does in the file photos, anyway. But who knows? Maybe he doesn't really look like that. I will find out soon enough.

I'll take it, I told the clerk. I'll do it. He nodded, pleased to have found another lawyer for a destitute killer, pleased to have made sure that all the killer's rights will be vindicated before he is led those last few steps to the green chamber and strapped into the oak chair.

McGuire. Jason Lee. Irish. Temperamental. Drink is gasoline splashed on the smouldering cinders of rage.

I went back to my law firm to explain about the foolishness I had gotten myself into.

The meeting takes place in a small half-cell, half-room on a short corridor off the cell block. It's called the conference room; it has a wood table painted black and two folding chairs. The windows are barred and the guard locks the conferees in before taking up station just outside.

Next door is the law library, a room of similar austerity but greater space, and furnished with a variety of legal materials. The library is where inmates go to research matters pertinent to their appeals—as well as they are able, given the incompleteness of the collection and the educational and intellectual limitations under which most of them labor.

Not too many years ago the library was a place the inmates went to search up some hope; now it's become stuffy with desperation. People aren't winning appeals anymore. They aren't winning stays. Instead they are being led away, one by one, through those heavy gray steel doors, and they aren't coming back. They disappear in the middle of the night, and a day or two or three later others are moved into their cells.

Jason is waiting in the conference room, dressed in his pale blue jumpsuit, hands cuffed, a manacle on his leg, when the door swings open about ten minutes before two. The guard mutters something to a man in a dark blue suit. The man is handsome in a mild way: dark hair cut short, chin and cheeks well shaved, eyes a clear blue. He could be anywhere from twenty-five years old to forty, Jason thinks, but probably closer to twenty-five. (In fact the man is thirty-three.)

"He's in here," says one of the guards, and shows the man into the conference room. "Been waiting for you for a while. Hey kid. This is your new lawyer. Bryan Delafield."

The lawyer looks apprehensive. Jason looks hostile. Bryan extends a hand.

"Hello, Jason," he says. The boy makes no move to complete the handshake. "I'm your new lawyer. I'll be handling your appeal."

"Guess I'll leave you two lovebirds alone," says the guard. The door clangs shut behind him, and Bryan feels the panic rising. He is locked up in prison with a brutal killer. There is no way out. The boy looks evil in a way not suggested in the photos. He takes a few deep breaths and

opens his briefcase. The officiousness settles him down a
little.

"Well," he says.

"What if I don't want an appeal?" Jason says. "What if I
don't want you here and I don't want no appeal and I just
want to get things over with?"

"You've got no choice, I'm afraid," says Bryan.
"Appeals of death sentences are automatic. State law." He
glances up from his papers. His client is staring at him
with amazingly green eyes: cat's eyes. Glow-in-the-dark
eyes. "Things OK here?" Bryan asks.

"Oh, yeah, terrific," Jason says. "I love it here."

"If there's a problem," Bryan says, "I'll talk to
somebody."

"There's no problem," Jason says.

Bryan draws a deep breath. "Maybe we should talk
about the case a little," he says.

"I did it," Jason says with an off-center grin. "I'm
guilty as sin. Blew them away. Right between the eyes." He
points a finger at Bryan and pulls the trigger.

"My understanding was that you used a knife," Bryan
says coolly. "Not a gun."

"I sure did," Jason says. "Mother was almost a foot
long. Still got 'em right between the eyes."

"What I'd like to do," Bryan says, "is emphasize a few
things in this appeal. Not raise points like scattershot, see
what I mean? I want to concentrate their attention on one
or two things."

"Like what?"

"Like you age, for instance. Seventeen at the time of
the offense, weren't you?"

"Something like that."

"And they beat you, didn't they?"

"Dunno."

"That's what your trial lawyer told me."

"Maybe they did. Maybe not."

"Both of them?"

"Why are you asking me these questions, man?" Jason says, suddenly irritable, suddenly vulnerable. He looks away—at the wall, at the small barred window.

"I'm sorry," Bryan says. "I'm not trying to make you angry. I just want as full an understanding as I can get of what happened that night. It'll help me. Help you."

"Don't want your help," Jason says. "Why don't you just leave me alone?"

They sit there in silence for a while. Soon the half hour will be up, Bryan will be shown out, Jason will be taken back to his cell to wait for dinner. Bryan thinks about the drive back, about the rain and the slick roads. If the weather is terrible he might have to stay overnight in the town of Warrensville, and that thought chills him.

"Did you read that book I sent you?" he asks at length.

"No."

"You should read it," Bryan says, at a loss for anything else to say. "It's a terrific story."

Jason says nothing.

"When you finish it I'll send you another."

"Thanks," Jason says. "I'll really be looking forward to that."

Snideness and bewilderment. Bryan is feeling the way he thinks Jason ought to be feeling. They have gotten nowhere. The guard knocks loudly and opens the door.

"Time's up,' he says. Bryan has already collected his things and put them back in his leather briefcase. Once again he extends his hand toward the boy.

"Well," he says, "I'll be in touch."

To his surprise Jason takes his hand.

"This way," says the guard, and Bryan is led out, leaving Jason behind in his handcuffs and manacle.

"You don't look well," Caroline says to me after she has tucked Jessie away for the night and we are lying side by side on our big bed, reading lamps on. She has been chuckling over a Barbara Pym novel; I appear to be engrossed in the trial transcript but all I am really thinking about is Warrensville. That face. "You've hardly said a thing since you got back from that place."

"I'm sorry," I say. "Just tired, I guess." I try to smile, and I caress her bare forearm. She is a kind woman, soft, gracious—always aware of my moods and uncertainties. I'm glad she's there next to me.

"Do you want to talk about it?" she says. "Nothing terrible happened, did it?"

"I don't know," I say, not sure if I don't want to talk about it or if something terrible happened. She waits patiently to see if I will continue. Vacantly I shuffle the pages of the transcript. My eyes glance over them: white pages with funny little black scratches on them, telling a story sordid in every respect. Yet the pages themselves aren't sordid in the least. They don't tell you a thing unless you look at them a certain way and with a certain knowledge. "It was pretty awful," I say.

Silently she takes my hand. Tell me, she says. Tell me about it.

"It's just that he's so young," I say. "I can't believe he's there. I can't believe he did what he did. You know what he said to me? 'I'm guilty as sin!' And he smiled like a maniac when he said it. I just don't understand, you know," I say, turning toward her and resting my chin on the top of her soft brown hair, "how a kid can turn out like that."

"It is scary," she agrees. "But there's nothing you can do about that now. All you can do is the best job you can for him. You don't even have to see him again."

Caroline is nothing if not the classic Monrovian: ignore all the nasty parts, she is telling me, and do a fabulous job in every other way. Tailor reality; limit it. This is the ethos that rules our fair city.

"I don't know that it's that simple," I say. "There's just something that bothers me about this case." I see those cat's eyes again and know I will dream about them tonight. That young, shapely face—no different from the faces you see wandering the campus atop the blue-jeaned, backpacked undergraduates studying chemistry or history. Not so different, really, from Caroline's face. Or mine.

Somehow she is stroking my dick now, kneading it back and forth between long fingers. It stays soft for a time, while my thoughts wander elsewhere, but she knows what she is doing, knows how to make it hard, and now it is hard. She goes down on me without a word, lips sliding up and down, up and down and around, and I feel it beginning to well up in me and gently I roll her onto her side and slip inside her. We grind a bit, ferociously, and she bites my ear and pinches my nipples and calls me a little fucker and I grunt and shoot and she grunts too.

"Sleep," she says, and kisses me on the lips.

"Sleep," I say, though I mean dream, and cat's eyes.

2

Ticktock, ticktock. The grandfather clock in the front hall about to strike seven. Time to get up for school. Time to climb into the shower, let the hot water run over your body. Wash hair, soap chest, clean between toes. Brush teeth. Put on blue jeans and T-shirt and Reeboks and zip up backpack with homework stuffed inside. Grab something to eat in the kitchen, mutter a thing or two to parents who sit sipping coffee and reading paper, exchange a bit of school gossip with brother. Then on with the jacket and out into the chill of a Columbia fall. If it is cold enough, wet hair will be frozen by the time you get to school.

Jason sat at the kitchen table in his underwear, eating cinnamon toast. He had already eaten two slices; another was browning in the toaster. The smell filled the kitchen; the noisy buzz of the timer. When the bread was golden he would sprinkle some brown sugar over it, add the cinnamon, and then spread the butter. The butter would melt into the sugar and cinnamon and there would be a gooey confection on top of the bread. It tasted quite good, like a glazed doughnut.

He had already drunk his orange juice, so he had his day's dose of vitamin C. Important to fight off colds in the winter months: his mother. He was also drinking coffee—a new development. Usually it was hot cocoa. But this morning he wanted to be awake, fully alert. It was a cold November morning, the sky a pale, arctic blue, frost on the front lawn, brittle and frozen leaves lining the gutters: the coffee felt good inside him. He had a pop quiz in American history later that morning.

Jason usually got up as late as possible, sometimes as late as a quarter to eight; he liked his sleep. Getting out of bed was always a struggle. Patrick, on the other hand, was an early riser: always up by seven, sometimes even earlier to go running. How could he be so cheerful so early in the morning? Patrick tried to be quiet but Jason always heard the sheets being peeled back, the sound of feet on the wood floor, the shuffle to the bathroom.

Mr. and Mrs. McGuire got up early, too: Donald to get to his construction company by eight, Kay to make sure everybody's day was starting with vitamin C and something from each of the four basic food groups.

Slowly Jason got up from the table and walked out into the living room. The wood floor was cold beneath his bare feet. He ran his hands along the side of his body, noted the sensuousness of it. The smooth, soft skin, taut over muscle. Cool to the touch. He wondered if he should do it again. He already did it once this morning, at six, sitting in his father's chair in the living room, the drapes wide open. That was after. A medium-sized damp stain on the front of his underwear. The ecstatic pulsing, like a heartbeat; fluid; the rhythm fading. Gone.

He decided not to. Instead he crept along the hallway

toward the bedrooms: all doors closed. His father's, his mother's, his and Patrick's, Colleen's. The clock struck seven, and he felt a chill. The sunlight was growing stronger now, yellow and fierce and low in the eastern sky. He went back to the kitchen and poured himself another cup of coffee.

Just about now, he thought.

Down the hall, the sound of a door opening. A creak, a whine. Mother. Shuffling slippers, a light knock. No answer. A louder knock, muffled words. Nothing. Another door squealing on its hinges as it slowly swung open. A terrific scream, sustained, piercing.

Check our room, too, he said, and absently felt the spot on his jockey shorts. He wasn't sure if it was blood. The toast popped up from the toaster. He got up to sprinkle the sugar and cinnamon and spread the butter.

At the police station Jason waited by himself in a little cell that smelled like piss. Drunks milling about talking to themselves, assorted other thugs, misfits, lunatics. Quite a town, Batavia. Eventually they would come to take his fingerprints and mugshots, then ask him what happened. Meantime he sat there. They had read him his Miranda rights right after they arrested him. Can you afford a lawyer? they asked. No. Then one will be appointed for you.

His mother was with the police in another part of the station, quivering like a trapped deer.

"All I can tell you, Officer," she said to a burly, middle-aged cop with a pad and pencil and crewcut, "is that I got up at seven and went to wake my husband and my sons. And I knocked on the boys' door and there was no answer and I knocked on my husband's and there was no answer so I called to him and nothing. You know, he's usually awake when I come in. So then I opened the door and there he was, you know—" She began to tremble violently and the officer murmured to reassure her.

"It's OK, there, ma'am," he said. "Just take some deep breaths."

"It's just that," she said, voice cracking, "it's just that I can't believe it happened. Things like this don't happen in Batavia." This was true: not in Batavia, peaceful little town, not too big, not too small, certainly far less dangerous than Monroe sixty miles east along Highway 52, full of crazed intellectuals and college students and public transportation. A nice town where people minded their own business.

"Well, ma'am," the officer said with a gentle shrug. "Maybe you can tell me what happened then."

"Of course," said Mrs. McGuire, struggling for her dignity. "Then. Then I went to the boys' door and opened it, and there he was. Patrick. You know, just . . . And Jason's bed was empty."

"And where was he?"

"In the kitchen. He must have heard me scream, and he asked if I was all right. I screamed and I was crying and then there he was in his underwear, with this dark stain on his underwear—that's all he was wearing. And he said, 'I guess you found 'em.' And I said, 'Yes, I did.' And he said, 'Why don't you call the police?' And so I did."

"He asked you to call?"

"Yes."

"Mmmm. Mrs. McGuire, forgive me, but there's one thing I don't quite understand."

"Yes?"

"You said that you got up and then went to your husband's room to wake him."

"That's right."

"You weren't in the same room?"

No reply.

"I apologize, ma'am."

"No, I wasn't."

"I see," he said uncertainly, as if wondering whether to push on. "You didn't actually see what happened, then."

"No, I didn't."

"I see." The officer shuffled some papers to conceal his embarrassment.

Some men came to Jason's cell and told him to take off all his clothes. They put the underwear in a plastic bag and searched him from head to toe. Fingers in his mouth, up his nose, between his fingers and toes, up his asshole. They told him to get dressed again and, after handcuffing him, took him to a brightly lighted room where his picture and fingerprints were taken.

"Now then, kid," said one of the men in a surprisingly gentle voice, "I'm Detective Lipinsky." He nodded to the other two, who withdrew from the room. Lipinsky was on the short side, dark hair and eyes, reassuringly lined face. The sort of man who had kids waiting at home. He said: "Let's you and me have a little talk. I just want to explain a little what's going to happen when your lawyer gets here. They told you that you're entitled to a lawyer. When they arrested you. Right?"

Jason nodded.

"I want to ask you some questions about what happened this morning. Try to figure out just what happened. Then we'll go see a judge—"

"You don't have to wait for my lawyer to get here," Jason said, mouth set in an absent sneer. "Whoever the fuck he is. Don't even want a lawyer. Told the cops that when they grabbed me. Don't even have to ask me questions. I'll tell you what happened."

Lipinsky sat there. He didn't say yes; he didn't say no. He just waited. Not for long.

"What happened," Jason said slowly, with apparent relish, "is that I killed them."

"Both of them."

"Yep."

"With the kitchen knife."

"You got it."

"I see," said Lipinsky. "What for?"

"I felt like it."

He went out of the room and a while later returned with a piece of paper. He explained what it was, asked Jason to read it and sign it. Jason signed. Didn't bother to read.

The lawyer's name was Edwards. Unkempt gray hair, spotty clothes, small sharp clear eyes. Vaguely parasitical; a whiff of beer about him? He came after lunch and asked Jason a number of questions. How are your grades? Skip classes? In trouble with the law before?

No.

Drink?

You know.

Drugs?

No.

Feel all right lately?

Fine.

I'm afraid, said Edwards, that there's fairly strong circumstantial evidence against you. The knife, the blood on your shorts, the fact that there was no sign of forced entry into the house. Still, it is up to the state to prove the case against you beyond a reasonable doubt. They're going to need better evidence than they've got.

They're not going to have much trouble getting it, I'm afraid, Jason said. I already told that detective guy I did it. Lipinsky. I think I even signed something.

The Batavia *Times-Courant* went up in smoke. TEEN SLAYS FATHER, BROTHER, read the headline the morning after the murder. "Motive sought in brutal knifings," said the subhead. The paper had established a reputation as the most emphatically law-and-order of the state's smaller newspapers, and its editorials were constantly calling for more severe treatment of criminals. Craven politicians feared nothing more than the scorn of the *Times-Courant*.

The town, Batavia, was bigger than a hamlet but smaller than a city. There was one high school, one fire station, two supermarkets; it was the sort of place where family names recurred over the decades on the lists of kindergarten enrollment. Where the parks on the summer Sundays were filled with picnicking families. The sort of place that gently, quietly, efficiently killed ambition.

"The father, Donald McGuire, was a foreman for Mackey Construction," said the *Times-Courant*. "He was born and raised in Batavia." Just the sort of man Batavians admired: a hard worker, a native, loyal to his hometown, his place: a family man. A big, hearty man whose parents emigrated from County Cork as tiny children, came to Batavia with their parents to make some kind of life.

"Patrick, 18, was a senior at Batavia High School and a member of the varsity track team." Patrick was handsome and popular and went out with the leader of the football cheerleaders.

"I can't believe it," the paper quoted her—Julie Something—as saying. "I just can't believe it. Patrick was such a great guy. There never seemed to be anything wrong with Jason. I mean, he went to school and everything. He got good grades. He and Patrick always seemed to get along."

Batavians, despite their rabid newspaper, were unused to crime. There was the occasional shoplifting or scuffle outside a downtown bar, but not much more. The few murders in the town's history were perpetrated by outsiders or drifters who simply happened to be in Batavia when they did the deed.

But Jason McGuire! said the women as they locked their doors at night, peered out windows, drew the drapes, stashed kitchen knives under their beds. Just in case. He always seemed like such a nice boy. So quiet and polite. He must have gone crazy. He must have been drunk. Solid young men of the sort they raised in Batavia didn't do things like this.

The *Times-Courant* published more details of the murder the following day. The size of the knife, where the victims were stabbed and how many times, how long the coroner thought it took them to die. Some of the more horrifying details were omitted in respect of the feelings of those more sensitive.

"They appear to have died rather quickly," said the coroner. "In a matter of a few seconds, I would guess. It was quite a long knife, and he is quite strong."

There were indistinct photos of the bedrooms where the two had been killed, the sheets tangled and stained, a portrait on the wall knocked to a crazy angle by the struggle. A photograph of Mrs. McGuire standing outside the police station, looking dazed.

"Mother calls teen killer 'a good boy,'" the caption

quoted her as saying. "'I don't know what we're going to do.'"

The tide of public opinion began to rise, like lava in a volcano. The shock, sympathy, disbelief gave way to something else. Anger, fury, hatred. Blood lust. The boy was not of them. Could not be. He was a cold-blooded killer. He had confessed. He was proud of it, the little bastard. Rumblings.

One night a few people stood outside the jail with picket signs: GIVE HIM A PRAYER AND PUT HIM IN THE CHAIR, one said. SHOCK A CON, said another. Their breath rose, delicate puffs in the chilly air. Christmas lights twinkling on the trees around them. The *Times-Courant* ran photos.

Thanksgiving Day. Jason lying on his back in his cell, digesting overcooked turkey and mashed potatoes. Bail had been set at $50,000: no way. One of the guards was listening to a college football game on the radio. Every now and then he cheered, or swore. The other jailmates shuffled around anxiously. The occasional belch, fart, yawn, sigh; the sound of someone writing.

He had been charged with two counts of murder. The state had given notice of its plans to seek the death penalty. Edwards had conveyed the news in his dispassionate way.

"That's no surprise, I'm afraid," he said. "Not with that paper screaming about the thing every day."

"Who cares?" Jason said.

"We'll get you off somehow."

"Somebody here to see you, kid," said the guard with the radio. He was clearly annoyed by the inconvenience of having to escort Jason to the visitor's room. This was

Thanksgiving, after all, and who the hell wanted to spend Thanksgiving with a bunch of criminals? Even if they were your family.

"Hello, Jason," said Mrs. McGuire. They had not seen each other in ten days, not since the judge set bail at what might as well have been $50 million. She had just not shown up.

"Mom." His face remained hard, she thought, but his voice was flat. Not bitterly flippant as it had been that horrible morning.

"Seeing how it was Thanksgiving," said Mrs. McGuire, "I thought I'd come visit. I'd have brought some turkey," she added, forcing a chuckle, "but I figured they'd search me and take it away."

"Where've you been?"

"Well, you know," she said uncertainly, glancing around the austere little room, the bars on the windows, the guards outside the door. "You know how it is. Little Colleen's not been feeling well, and I haven't had the time."

"That's all right," he said. "I don't really care."

"Oh Jason," she said. "Don't say that. I'm sorry. I've thought about coming. It's just that . . . you know."

"Yeah."

"Are they treating you well, at least?"

"Oh, yeah," he said. "The best."

"That's good," she said, fumbling. This was not her son, not the boy she'd thought she'd raised. "That's good."

"Yeah."

"Is there anything I can do for you?"

"Yeah," he said with a smile. "You can tell them why I did it."

She looked him straight in the eye, then looked away.

"I should have murdered you, too," he said.

She pretended that she hadn't heard this, or that he

hadn't said it. "Don't worry," she said. "I hear Edwards is a mighty fine lawyer. He'll get you off somehow."

"He's a drunk," he said. "But it doesn't matter. I've already admitted the whole thing." He laughed at her expression of shock. "The only thing I haven't told them is what the blood looked like when it came out of their necks. What it felt like. Do you want me to tell you? Then you can testify, too. OK?"

"Jason," she said, as though choking on a crust of bread. "Please."

A pause. He ran both hands through his hair, as though he'd just stepped out of the shower. She dabbed at her lips with a handkerchief.

"How is Colleen now?" he said.

"Much better. Much better. Of course she misses you," said Mrs. McGuire. "I miss you. I want you out of here."

"Don't be so sure," he said, then, "Tell her hi for me, will you?"

"I will."

"Oh, Jason," she said to him, and he thought she was about to burst into tears. But she didn't. "I want you to know how much I love you. Do you know that?"

"You don't love me," he said. "You can't."

"But I do."

"You should have stopped me," he said.

"I didn't know how."

"I'm glad they're dead, anyway," he said, rearranging the sleeves on his jail clothes. "That's something to be thankful for."

Mrs. McGuire hung her head.

"I'm glad I didn't wake you up," he said. "I tried to be as quiet as I could."

"I better go," she said. "I left Colleen at the Schwenns'."

"Is it that late already?" he said in mock excitement.

"I'm so sorry, Mom. The time just got away. Please tell Colleen I miss her," he said, and then, "Guard!"

She tried to touch him over the table, but he snorted and said something she couldn't make out. The guard came and led her away, out into the late afternoon, where it had begun to snow. Hard, brilliant little flakes swirling from the black sky. There was a light dusting on the windshield of her car. She brushed the flakes away.

Jason was lead back to his cell.

"God you missed a fantastic play," said the guard. "Fake field-goal attempt and a 22-yard pass for a touchdown."

"Really."

3

Writing this brief—it's a relief after my meeting with that kid. I'd rather be boxed up in the library, surrounded by musty old volumes of statute books and regional reporters, than have "client contacts" that leave me sleepless. Any day. They say lawyers are sociopaths and I've always thought that's true—too much of the gladiator instinct, too little sense of the tiny human dramas from which legal doctrine is shaped—but I've never thought I was. Now I find comfort in the solitude, the hours spent away from the office, the family, the eyes of my cherub killer. There is pleasure in the numbness of legal research, the negative pleasure of knowing that I am managing to avoid pain.

I met Caroline in this very law library. I was a second-year law student at the University of Columbia School of Law; she was an undergraduate working behind the checkout desk. I was always checking out this or that hornbook from her—Torts, Contracts, Property, Property, and more Property—and after a while she would hand the heavy volumes to me with a little laugh. I felt like a loser and thought she, shrewd, sarcastic undergraduate, swathed in her Lands' End yachting sweaters, was chuckling at my inability to learn the law from the material the professors assigned us. A nerdy law student, and not even a successful one. After about four months of these tiny encounters, of pathetically subsisting on them, I asked her out and she said yes. Quite the triumph for a guy who hadn't seen much dating action since the second grade.

We ended up going to a bar on University where all the law students hung out. Everybody talking about assumption of risk and equitable estoppel and who fucked up reciting that day. What the hot firms were. How much they were paying. Whether it was worthwhile to do a clerkship, and, if so, with a U.S. district judge or a justice of the state supreme court. (It went without saying that virtually everybody wanted to stay in Monroe, but it was an overlawyered town even then and most of us were resigned to leaving.) We ordered hamburgers and beer and sat down to talk. We ended up talking most of the evening, and I walked her home and gave her a peck on the lips. It was exhilarating, and for the first time in a long time I walked home along University—the fast way—instead of along the lakeshore.

It was sheer serendipity. I didn't expect anything to come of it.

You try to raise as many issues as you can in these appeals. You never know what might stick—probably nothing, but possibly the most improbable argument. That's what they tell me, the guys who've done a lot of death-penalty appeals before. Just blast out anything you can make a case for. Blunderbuss appellate argument. Not exactly my precise, anal-retentive style, in which everything must be just so, but a life hangs in the balance. People from the Death Penalty Project call from time to time to make sure that I'm not cracking up or getting squeamish about pushing the thinner claims.

It's not that I dislike Jason. Why should I like him, or not? I don't really have strong feelings either way. I'm not supposed to. The murders were ghastly, of course, but all murders are. My job is not to get emotional. My job is to think, and to see that justice is done.

I must admit that I feel a little more hesitant about handling this boy's appeal than I did before I met him. Perhaps meeting him was a mistake. I've always thought that kids who killed their parents had some good reason for doing it: physical abuse or something like that. The parent making the kid's life unbearable. And the kid being genuinely remorseful afterward.

But my heart tells me that's not what's going on here. There are teenagers who've killed their parents when they didn't get a big enough raise in their allowance or weren't allowed to use the family car. Jason is one of these—a truly nutty killer.

Still, there's a case to be made—a better case than most. There's a strong possibility that the confession to Detective Lipinsky was coerced. And the prosecutor showed the jury police photos of the bodies in all their glory—totally unnecessary and inflammatory. It's a case I can win.

To be honest: this is not a case in which one's skin crawls at an obvious injustice. I don't really believe the boy has been treated unfairly, or cheated of some right, or in some other way deprived of the opportunity to make his case. There isn't much you can say against the claim that here's a killer who deserves whatever he gets. He admitted everything, shows no remorse, smiles when you ask him about it. But serious errors were committed, and it's not exactly cheating our system of justice to get the boy a life sentence.

The troubling question, of course, is why he did it. The murders just don't make sense. This is totally irrelevant to the appeal, because the case against Jason didn't depend on the state's ability to establish a motive. He admitted everything in that stupid confession, which I cannot understand why he made. Still, one would like to know.

"I don't understand why you didn't call him as a witness," I told his trial lawyer, Edwards, over lunch a few days ago. "You could have at least gotten some sympathy from the jury. He might have given some clue as to why he did it."

"Unless he's the total monster I think he is," Edwards said through bites of his roast beef sandwich and swigs of beer. "That confession was a bit of a problem, you know. He couldn't very well deny it. Besides, he told me he would refuse to take the stand. So."

"Why?"

"You ask him," said Edwards. "He wouldn't give me a reason."

"There's something I've been very curious about," I said.

"Why. I suppose it was drugs or something. You know how kids are nowadays. They think they're entitled to everything. The old man wouldn't spring for a Corvette, for all I know. Doesn't much matter at this point. Don't forget he's a psycho."

"He wouldn't tell you?"

"Not a word."

"Did you ask him?"

"Of course I asked him," he said, a trace of irritation in his voice.

"Nothing?"

"Not a peep. Smiled and told me he just felt like it and never to ask him that fucking question again because he wasn't going to answer it. I quote."

"Your gut feeling?"

"He's a devil, Bryan, that's all I can tell you," Edwards said with a sigh and another swig of beer. "He's not like you and me. I don't know where he came from or what made him the way he is, but he's callous and dangerous. To tell you the truth, I'm not all that sorry I lost."

To tell you the truth: the thought of this boy, Jason, killing his father and brother, alternately excites and appalls me. It's so vivid, life and death. I shouldn't feel this way, I know. Maybe it's just the foreignness of it that gives the thrill. The electric animalness. When I was seventeen I was afraid to masturbate and every night after dinner my parents made me study until 10, when I got to watch the news before going to bed. I got my As and Bs and was on my way to college, law school, marriage, children, the nice house, the regard of my peers.

Jason's passion dazzles. That's what it was: passion. It couldn't be anything else. He absolutely stabbed the hell out of them, hated them; and I know he's not crazy, that he didn't stab mechanically like those loonies who think they're printing presses, making a perfectly neat line of wounds across the neck, down the shoulder, onto the rumpled expanse of bedsheet. He knew just what he was doing.

Mind wandering. Time to go. I pass the loan desk on my way out—the desk where I first saw Caroline nine years ago. There's a young guy standing there now. I smile anyway, and say hello.

*   *   *

Jessie is riding her bike around the driveway when I pull in just before ten. Caroline is sitting on the front steps watching her and calling out the occasional word of encouragement.

"Hi," she says while Jessie wobbles around us. "Late night."

"Yes," I say. "I'm sorry."

"We saved you some dinner," she says. "Macaroni and cheese and some broccoli. I'll heat it up."

"Thanks," I say, and follow her just inside, where we embrace briefly and kiss. She smells like Coast. "I'll stay here a minute and watch her." I take off my jacket, loosen the tie, and sit down on the stoop. Jessie pedals by, saying, "Watch, Daddy!" and taking her hands off the handlebars. I am tempted to tell her to knock it off, that it's dangerous, but before I can she's ridden onto the lawn and taken a tumble.

"Are you all right?" I ask as I hurry to her side. The grass is damp and her little skirt is stained with mud. The bike lies in a heap.

"Fine," she says, already vaguely embarrassed, though only four years old, that her father treats her like a baby. Of course she is a baby: I still see her sometimes as the angry red week-old bundle we brought home from the hospital, fists knotted, quivering wail like a police siren.

"Bryan!" Caroline calls from the kitchen. "Dinner's ready. Jessie! Bedtime."

"I want to stay up with you," she says. "All right?"

"Only for a little while," I say. "While I eat. Then you have to go to bed." She pouts a little but resigns herself to this modest victory. She has always hated to go to bed, and only in the last few months has she given up her habit of breaking into our bedroom at five in the morning to lodge herself between us.

"The McGuire thing?" Caroline says.

"Yeah," I say, as I sit down and start in on the macaroni and broccoli. "Mmmm."

"What's McGuire?" Jessie says.

"Someone I work for," I say.

"Is he important?"

"Not really," I say, and then, because this doesn't seem to me to be an entirely satisfactory answer (though she accepts it): "He's a young man who needs my help."

"Is he hurt?"

"Jessie," Caroline says, "bedtime."

"He's in trouble," I say.

"Did he do something bad?"

"I'm afraid so."

"Do you like him?"

"Jessie."

"I don't really know," I say. "I don't really know him."

"I hope he's all right," she says as Caroline scoops her up in her arms. "I hope you can help him."

"So do I, precious," I say, and kiss her on her forehead as her mother holds her. "I'll come in later and tuck you in."

"I'll be asleep by then," she says sensibly, and they march off.

"I'll be right back," says Caroline, and I sit down to finish the rest of the macaroni and cheese.

We sit in front of the television for a while—me in an easy chair, Caroline on the sofa. The sound is turned way down, and the images—network promos, an ad for wine coolers, one for the state fair, a snippet from the upcoming news broadcast—flash by silently.

"I'm a little worried about you," she says.

"Why?"

"Because of Mr. McGuire, I guess," she says.

"*Mr.* McGuire is barely out of diapers," I say. "His name is Jason. Anyway I thought you disapproved of the death penalty. You should be thrilled that someone—me of all people—is working feverishly to save the life of a convicted killer."

"I suppose you're right," she says with a sigh. A moment of Monrovian angst sets in: Ideals v. Reality. The never-ending struggle. I suppress a smile. "But I'm not thrilled," she continues. "I don't like to see you coming home after a twelve-hour day all pale and exhausted. Jessie kept asking where you were."

"It's not going to be that bad," I tell her. "Once I get the research done, I can do the writing here. That's all. Then all I have to do is give the oral argument and that's it. Justice is served."

"You don't have to go back to that prison? I worried all day."

"No plans," I say.

She seems mildly satisfied by this. I pick up the remote control and turn up the sound.

"... for an execution scheduled next week at the state prison in Warrensville," says the anchor, a young woman. "Peter Fletcher has more."

There it is: the walls, the wire, the grim gray little buildings. Stock footage of the green chamber, the chair. Warden Fred Riley explaining about the last meal, etc. I feel my pulse leap. Who is it?

"... as last-minute appeals proceed for convicted murderer Alpha Lynaugh," says Peter Fletcher. "From Warrensville, Peter Fletcher, Channel 3 News."

"Thank you, Peter," says the anchor at the conclusion of the videotaped report. "And coming up—the five-day weather outlook. Ed Quigg will have all the steamy details."

It's not Jason. How could it be? I haven't even saved him yet. "God," I say.

"Let's go to bed. Please?" says Caroline.

She is asleep and I am lying there wide awake. Every now and then she snores or snorts, or extends an arm toward me or rolls this way or that. These sounds fill me with envy: the sounds of untroubled sleep. Every aspect of the bedroom seems to annoy tonight. The light of the digital alarm clocks. The soft hush of cooled air blowing in from the central air conditioner. The muted blue moonlight.

At the moment I feel as though I do not love anything. I don't feel anything other than frustration that I can't fall asleep and leave this all behind. This appeal, Jason. The family waiting here loyally for me to come home and complete the picture. The First National Bank of Monroe, which is getting upset with the firm because the lawyer they rely on most often—me—is, for the time being, available only on a limited basis.

I lie back on the pillows, arms folded behind my head, and try to take deep breaths. I feel short-winded. I haven't swum in a week. I haven't played squash since Memorial Day. Fat accretes. I run a hand down the front of my body, over my chest and belly, monitoring the signs of deterioration. I haven't even been all that hungry lately.

Of course I love Caroline. Have ever since we started to go out. Eight years. She gave up graduate school to marry me, gave up her physical therapist job at the U. of C. Clinics to have Jessie. How can I not love her? She was willing to do all that when I would have settled for a dog.

Speaking of which. This weekend we will take Jessie to the zoo, which does not have a panda. She has already told her mother that she wants a panda for Christmas.

"Only a small one," she says in a small voice. Caroline has explained the difficulties, but it is not always easy to make a four year old understand these things. I've heard that pandas aren't as sweet as they look, anyway. And where would we get all that bamboo for them to eat? Funny word. Sleep at last.

4

It's almost midnight. Jason is wide awake, mind and body coiled like a jungle animal's. Sleep impossible. Stirrings down the cell block a ways. Anxious gossip up and down the row. Hysteria rising: denial, fury, terror, despair.

"They're going to do it," says a voice.

"Bastards."

"Are you sure?"

"They shaved his head this morning."

"Looked like an eight ball."

"Round and shiny."

Alpha Lynaugh's cell was near Jason's: on the same side but farther down. Toward the steel doors. He was moved away a week ago to a special cell for the deathwatch. The day before, they move you to another cell just feet from Gretchen. There you wait. Pray with the chaplain. Listen for the footsteps.

Jason feels an irrational thrill of relief that his cell is farther away from the doors than Alpha's was, as though being drawn through them is simply a matter of physical proximity. Like the window of a jet plane giving way and the passengers sitting nearest it being sucked out.

Alpha Lynaugh is a big man, fortyish, hair long and braided like a Rastafarian's. Graying. Heavy black spectacles like Woody Allen's. Word is that he was some kind of professor; taught at a college up north. They have virtually nothing in common, Jason and Alpha. But somehow the man became the only friend Jason had on the row, and already Jason misses him.

This is the first such occasion since Jason arrived two months ago. He is still a virgin. Will I hear anything? he wonders. Will I smell anything? Encounters with Gretchen are reputed to be unpleasant. Grisly. The guards talk about it all the time, when it's late at night and they're feeling mean. They talk about the stench of burning flesh, the horrible strains and quivers, the smoke rising from the arms, the sizzling, the electrodes that occasionally fail and send sparks showering around the green chamber.

They talk about the witnesses who throw up or pass out. They talk about the guy in the chair pissing and shitting in his pants; the burn marks all over his body when they finally turn the power off and the doctor pronounces him dead and they unstrap him and load him onto the stretcher for the short trip to the prison morgue. The autopsy must wait until the body cools off; the brain boils, they say, the liver is too hot to touch.

They talk about all these things loudly, laughing, so none of the prisoners can sleep.

"Sweet dreams, you fuckin' killers," they sometimes say when the shift changes. "Fuckin' scum of the earth."

Sometimes they say nothing. Some of them are even nice.

There's no sound down the cell block. Jason wonders what time it is, exactly. The death warrant, signed by the governor, specifies that the sentence is to be executed sometime between midnight and dawn within a period of three or four days, but the warden likes to get it over with as quickly as possible so people can go home. So far as anyone can remember, these things always happen just past midnight.

"It's happenin'," says someone down the block in a voice edged with madness. "I just know it. Right now, the damn bastards. Alpha!" he screams, and a guard quickly appears and tells him to shut up.

"It ain't even midnight yet," says another inmate in a reasonable voice. In fact it's now several minutes past midnight.

The minutes tick by like all the other minutes in this place. Silence.

Outside the prison gates two groups of perhaps a dozen people have gathered. One group carry lighted candles. The other carry placards that read "Let 'em have it" or "Eye for an eye." The two groups stay separated. They act as though the other weren't there. And they wait.

At about half past midnight a dark blue sedan drives up to the gate and an assistant warden gets out.

"It's all over, folks," he says through a megaphone. "12:21 A.M. Why don't you all go home? That's what I'm going to do," he says to one of the guards as he gets back in the car and they drive away.

The placard bearers whoop for a little while but gradually disperse. The candle bearers stand silently before the gates, heads bowed or raised to the heavens. One by one their candles burn out, and they melt away into the darkness.

Jason sees none of this.

"What time is it?" he says aloud, to no one in particular. He knows there's a guard at each end of the cell block, that each guard has a watch; but neither says anything.

"Must be about twelve thirty," someone in another cell says.

"Twelve twenty-six," says someone else.

No smell. No sizzling. No sparks. Maybe it's not happening. Maybe it never really happens, Jason thinks wildly. Maybe there is no Grisly Gretchen after all.

"The Lord is my shepherd—" someone begins.

"Shut the fuck up," shouts someone else, at the far end of the cell block. "Stuff your fuckin' God. He ain't goin' to do nothin' for us."

"—I shall not want—"

Jason tries to picture Alpha with his head shaved. He can't get the image of the eight ball out of his mind. The prayer goes on incoherently. There is a clanging at the end of the cell block: the double steel doors. The warden strides through without saying a word, guards in front and behind. Clomp clomp clomp go the heavy black shoes. He disappears into another part of the prison without making so much as a gesture. The reporters are waiting. The guards behind him linger.

"All over," one of them more or less announces. "Twelve twenty-one. Ten minutes ago. He went right away. Shrimp and steak for his last meal."

His voice is flat, devoid of malice or sympathy or any other emotion. He simply reports the facts. I suggest you all get to sleep, he says, and then leaves.

Jason lies there a while, in the dark. He thinks about the man shouting out the Lord's Prayer. He thinks about Alpha's head shaved bald. About his own. The cue ball. Do they let you look in a mirror after they're done? Do they shave you all over? Do they do your crotch, too? Maybe if you're a rapist they stick the electrode there. Or, if you've been really bad, up your ass. Will they grant his last wish? He has a particular desire. A dirty dream. Eventually he falls asleep hoping to dream it.

"The most important thing you have to remember," said Alpha Lynaugh, "is not to be afraid. There is nothing to be afraid of." He sounded like a preacher sometimes, other times like a teacher, but he commanded Jason's attention all the same. He had struck up a conversation with Jason only a few days after the boy had been installed in his cell. They talked even though they could not see each other, even though their hands were wrapped around steel bars. It didn't take Alpha more than a week to arrange a meeting in the exercise yard.

"I'm not afraid."

"Bullshit," said Alpha. "Of course you are. We all are. That's the great battle we all fight."

He went on doing his jumping jacks while Jason stretched. Alpha was overweight, and he huffed and puffed from the exertion. Three guards watched them stonily. It was not common practice for death-row inmates to be allowed to exercise together, but Alpha had nurtured understandings with most of the guards on the row. He usually could get done what he wanted to get done.

They flopped to the ground to do their isometrics. This was Jason's idea: he was the fitness expert.

"The point is," Alpha continued, "that the state is getting ready to commit the gravest of injustices against us. They are the murderers now, plotting every last detail of their hideous crimes. You must be indignant, and use your indignation. It will give you strength. Do you understand? Do you see what I mean?"

"I don't know," Jason admitted.

"You must not let them control you, dominate your spirit!" he said. "You must not! They are the criminals, not you. Why, boy," he said, turning a quieter scrutiny suddenly to Jason, "you're just a child. What in the name of Jesus Christ are you doing here?"

"I killed my father and brother."

"Ah," said Alpha. "Family troubles. I killed a man while I was holding up a liquor store. Didn't even mean to shoot the poor bastard, but he made a move. Scared me. I shit my pants after I did it. Just like a baby. Thought they'd find me just from the smell." He laughed a little.

"I thought you taught college."

Alpha chuckled again. "Almost," he said. "Tenth-grade English. I taught *Tom Sawyer* and *Huck Finn* to kids like you."

"Why did you rob the liquor store?"

"Couldn't afford to pay for it," he said. "Got fired. 'Complaints about your job performance,' they said. 'Reports of liquor on your breath.' All true, I'm sad to say. Why did you kill them?"

"Felt like it."

"Hmmm," Alpha said. "Just like that."

"Yeah."

"None of my business, is it?"

"Right."

"Well," Alpha said with a sigh, "I never claimed to understand families. You don't seem like a cold-blooded killer, though."

"Thanks," Jason said. "I am."

"I guess so."

One of the guards squashed his cigarette butt under the heel of his boot and told them to get their asses back inside.

"You got yourself a lawyer?" Alpha asked as they walked to the cell block.

"Guy f.om Monroe," Jason said. "He's supposed to be hot shit. Haven't met him yet. Don't even know his name."

"That's good, that's good," Alpha said. "You've got to have a good lawyer. You've got a good shot of getting out of here, Jason, I mean that," he said. "You're too young, too young. What the hell do they think they're doing, sending a kid here?"

"I knifed the hell out of them," Jason said. "You should have seen the blood."

"Don't talk smart," Alpha snapped. "I've seen plenty of blood and it's not pretty. Don't be a smartass. Just be damn glad you've got a lawyer who if he has a brain in his head will get you out of here."

"I don't want to get out of here."

"Of course you fuckin' want to get out of here. Everybody does."

Bloody dawn seeps through the bars, down into the cell. Jason stirs. Nightmares. Father with a shaved head. Patrick sitting in Gretchen. A loud fart rips the morning stillness.

"You do that in Gretchen," the guard says loudly, "you'll set the whole damn place on fire."

"Fuck you," someone says softly.

"What'd I hear?" says the guard, struggling up from his chair. "Who said that?"

Silence. He begins to stride down the corridor dividing the cells, looking speculatively in each, fingering his gun, his club, reaching out once or twice to rattle the bars.

"It was you, wasn't it, nigger boy?"

No reply.

"Thought I wouldn't recognize your nigger voice, didn't you? Stupid nigger. Can't hardly talk, can you, boy? Shit, man, no wonder you're in there. Too fuckin' stupid to get away." He laughs: a high-pitched, grating noise, like a dying coffee grinder. "I guess you just ain't going to get no breakfast this morning, nigger," he says agreeably, and reaches out to rattle the bars of the unseen cage.

Fuck you, Jason thinks.

There is the sound of a scuffle.

"Hey!" says the guard. "Let go. Let go of me, damn you!" Fear rising in his voice. The other guard hurries from the far end of the cell block to aid his comrade.

"I slit twenty throats," says a black voice in a menacing hiss. "I ever get the chance, I'll slit yours too."

There is the awful clanging sound of a billy club being beaten on the metal bars.

"You ain't never going to get the chance, nigger," says the second guard. "You'll be frying in that chair like a side of black bacon before you ever get the chance."

The black voice laughs. The first guard walks away as resolutely as he can. He passes Jason's cell without looking in either direction, as though he were marching in a parade.

Breakfast is on its way, but Jason does not want muffins and cereal and orange juice. He doesn't even want shrimp and steak. He doesn't want anything.

Dear Mom,

It's cloudy this morning and kind of hot. I don't feel like doing anything and I'm not hungry. What's it like there?

I wish you could come visit me sometime. With Colleen. I know it's a lot to ask for. I hope you're living in a better place. In a way, this is a better place for me.

I know you did what you had to do. I hope you can see that I did what I had to, too. Maybe that doesn't make sense, but it does to me. I know you think I'm bad but I'm not really. It's hard to explain.

They took my friend Alpha away last night. He was the guy I told you about. I didn't even get a chance to say good-bye.

Please come and visit me if you can afford it. Maybe there are cheap plane fares. Tell Colleen I love her. And I love you and miss you.

Your son,
Jason

5

The trial didn't amount to much, despite the *Times-Courant*'s robust coverage. Huge headlines—TEEN SLAYER TO TRIAL; MOM: 'I DON'T KNOW WHAT HAPPENED'; STATE SEEKS DEATH PENALTY IN SLAYINGS—along with photos of the accused, the surviving members of his family, the prosecutor, Grisly Gretchen.

Readers of the *Times-Courant* were treated to a spectacle: a dance of death. But things were different in Judge Thomas P. Schulz's courtroom.

This was elegantly paneled and high-ceilinged, on the second floor of the county building in the heart of Batavia. A building built before the turn of the century from locally quarried flagstone. A room that smelled of polish and tradition, in which voices were seldom raised. Tall windows in deep wells that looked out on the town square, the elms, the rose beds. A room in which Judge Schulz, gray-haired and courtly, sat on his raised bench and asked the occasional question of counsel, made the occasional ruling on a hearsay objection, sentenced the occasional drunk driver to three months' rehabilitation. Civilized, orderly; like the town itself.

Jason had wanted to plead guilty and get it all over with, but Edwards was a dedicated lawyer and at last, after wearing down the boy's resistance, convinced him to plead not guilty.

"They won't give up the death penalty even if you plead," he said, "so we might as well go to trial. That confession thing, that he went ahead and questioned you when I wasn't there, that's going to kill them."

"I don't really give a shit," Jason said.

Edwards ignored his client. He was a competent lawyer, not brilliant but dogged, who had made a comfortable living from court appointments and collection work. He knew what he was doing in the criminal law, and while he didn't care much for Jason personally, his professional instinct was engaged by what appeared to be serious difficulties in the state's case. This was, for him, the law's true appeal—the attempt to square the doctrine with the facts of a particular case. He was accustomed to representing unsavory clients and had long ago learned the art of suppressing his feelings about them.

"The defendant, Jason Lee McGuire, pleads not guilty, Your Honor," he said at the outset of the trial.

The prosecutor was Joseph D'Orsino. His first move was to ask that Jason's confession be read into the record.

"Objection!" cried Edwards. "Your Honor, I object. That 'confession,' as Mr. D'Orsino calls it, was taken from my client before he had a chance to speak with his attorney."

"He didn't want an attorney, Your Honor," said D'Orsino. He was gearing up to run for mayor and was interested in currying favor with the *Times-Courant*. Easy death-penalty cases were like $5,000 contributions to his campaign, and this was the biggest easy of them all. "He said so."

"I'm afraid I'm going to have to overrule, Counsel," said Judge Schulz. "There's been no suggestion that the confession was anything but voluntary."

"Your Honor," said Edwards, "I beg to differ."

The state called Kay McGuire.

"Mrs. McGuire," D'Orsino began in a tone of hushed deference, "you were at home on that morning, were you not?"

"Yes, I was."

"Can you tell the court what happened?"

"Well," Mrs. McGuire began, "I woke up at my usual time—seven in the morning, the alarm goes off then—and I got out of bed and went to wake my husband and the boys."

"Your husband slept in another room."

"That's right," said Mrs. McGuire. She cast an uneasy glance at the judge. "That's right. Anyway I went to wake them and I knocked on the boys' door and there was no answer and I knocked again and nothing so I went to my husband's door and knocked and nothing. Then I opened the door and there he was, lying there—"

She paused. D'Orsino waited what seemed to be a discreet interval, then said: "Mrs. McGuire? What then?"

"I'm sorry," she said, taking several deep breaths. "I screamed and started crying and went to the kitchen and Jason was sitting there at the table in his underwear, with blood all over them and a bloody knife in the sink, and he said, 'I guess you found them.'"

"Could you repeat that last sentence, ma'am?"

"He said, 'I guess you found them.'"

Cross-exam.

"Mrs. McGuire," said Edwards, "you testified that you and your husband slept in separate bedrooms."

"Objection!" shouted D'Orsino. "Irrelevant."

"I haven't even asked the question yet, Your Honor."

"Proceed."

"Was this a temporary arrangement or a permanent one?"

"Objection. Irrelevant."

"Overruled. Please answer the question, Mrs. McGuire."

"Permanent, I guess," said Mrs. McGuire.

"For how long had you and your husband slept apart?"

"Objection. Your Honor, this is irrelevant and way out of line."

"I'll give you a little more leeway, Mr. Edwards," said Judge Schulz. "But get to the point."

"Oh, I don't know," she said in a small voice. "Four years, I guess. Maybe longer."

"Why did you sleep apart?"

"Objection, Your Honor!"

"I'm afraid I'll have to sustain this one. Mr. Edwards, I don't see where you're going with this."

"If you weren't in your husband's bedroom," said Edwards, "then you couldn't have actually *seen* anything, could you, Mrs. McGuire? The actual killings, I mean."

"No."

"She never said she did, Counsel."

"Mrs. McGuire, did Jason ever skip school?"

"Not that I know of," she said. "No."

"If he had, would you have had any way to know about it?"

"They put that kind of thing on your report card, I guess."

"And Jason's report cards never indicated skips?"

"No."

"He always showed you his report cards?"

"Yes, he did. I had to sign them."

"How were his grades?"

"You know. Mostly Cs and Bs. Sometimes an A."

"And he swam on the varsity team."

"That's right."

"Did you ever see him do violence before?"

"No, sir," she said. "He was always very gentle."

"He never fought with his father?"

"No."

"His brother?"

"No."

"They were close?"

A pause.

"They weren't exactly friends," she said carefully. "But brothers are like that. Mostly I guess they ignored each other."

"Thank you, Mrs. McGuire."

Edwards lost most of his motions. It had been a bad sign in the pretrial hearing when Judge Schulz granted D'Orsino's motion that Jason stand trial as an adult.

"It's just the brutality of it all," said the judge. "I mean, in absolute cold blood. Unprovoked. His brother and his father. He's not a little boy, Counsel."

"Judge," said Edwards, "that's exactly what he is."

Despite Jason's objections, little Colleen McGuire took the stand. Edwards had talked to her soon after the murders and, as he told Jason, "wanted to play a hunch."

"I don't want you fooling with my sister," Jason said. "She's just a little girl."

"She says the old man beat up on you and your brother. That your brother beat up on you."

"Fuck that. I've told you. No way. She can't tell you a thing. She doesn't know what she's talking about."

"We'll see," said Edwards. Jason grunted with disgust.

"Will you tell us how old you are, Colleen?" Edwards asked.

The girl tugged at her braided blond hair and said, "Nine. Ten in June."

"So you're in the fourth grade."

"Yes."

"Colleen, can you tell us a little bit about your father and your brothers?"

"Well," she said slowly, "they watched baseball a lot on TV."

"Did they get along?"

"I guess."

"Did your dad ever yell at them?"

"Sometimes," she said. "If he was mad."

"When was he mad?"

"When they did something he didn't like. You know. Broke something."

"Did he punish them?"

"He wouldn't always let them drive the car," she said. "If he was mad at them. Sometimes he wouldn't give them their allowance."

"Did he ever hit them?"

"No," she said hesitantly.

"You're sure," Edwards said with a smile. "He never laid a hand on them."

"I'm not sure," she said.

"What are you not sure about?"

"Sometimes he would go to their room—"

"Jason and Patrick's?"

"Yes. He would go in there and it sounded funny."

"Like what?"

"Like he was hitting them."

"Objection!" D'Orsino cried. "Speculation."

"I'm asking the witness to described what she heard, Your Honor."

"Overruled," said the judge.

"What did the noises sound like?"

"I don't know," she said, squirming in the witness box. "Like he was hurting them."

"Violent."

"Yes."

"When did you hear these noises, Colleen?"

"I don't know," she said. "Lots of times."

"When he was mad at them?"

"Yes, sometimes," she said. "No special time."

D'Orsino's cross-exam was brief.

"Colleen," he said, "did you ever *see* your father hit either of your brothers?"

"No."

"You never saw him touch either one of them."

"No."

"Did he ever shout at them?"

"Well, sometimes he got mad when they took the car or something and they weren't supposed to."

"Did he threaten them? Did he say he was going to hurt them?"

"No."

"Did either Jason or Patrick ever tell you that your father was hurting them or telling them he was going to hurt them?"

"No."

"Did he ever hurt you, Colleen? Hit you?"

"No."

"Thank you, Colleen. No further questions, Your Honor."

"What the hell was going on in there?" Edwards whispered to Jason.

"Nothing," he said. "She's making it all up."

"I would like to remind the jury," D'Orsino said, "that the defendant has confessed to both killings in some detail."

The jury needed less than an hour to convict Jason on both counts of capital murder.

At the sentencing phase of the trial, D'Orsino showed the jury police photos of the bodies as they were discovered. Bloody and harsh, limbs askew, white flesh, faces locked in shock. And, of course, the mutilations. The jurors gasped audibly at the sight. Edwards snapped his pencil in half.

"Shit," he said under his breath. He had objected bitterly to the introduction of the photos as evidence, but the judge concluded that the jurors were entitled to consider these details of the crime as they weighed whether Jason should be sentenced to death or life in prison. The state was basing part of its death-penalty argument on the claim that the murders were unusually ghastly.

"Don't sweat it, man," Jason said. "That's what it really looked like. Be glad you weren't there."

D'Orsino also introduced Jason's alarm clock, which had been seized the morning of the murders. The alarm was set to go off at 5:20. This, D'Orsino told the jurors, was proof that the murders were planned, coldly, methodically.

"We may not know why he did it," he said, "but we know that he *planned* to do it. He didn't just fly off the handle in a rage and kill them. He *planned* to do it. He planned it all out."

Edwards spoke about Jason's respectable grades, his good attendance record, his credible performance on the high school swim team. Mostly he spoke about his youth—a theme he returned to time and again.

"You have found that my client committed these terrible acts, and we do not question that finding," he said. "But what we must not forget was that this was a young boy. A schoolboy in whose mind and life something has gone terribly wrong. He should be punished; of course he should be. He should be punished severely. He deserves that. But ladies and gentlemen of the jury, he does not deserve to die. To condemn him to the electric chair is to say: 'There is no hope for you. You are worthless, irredeemable. Begone.'

"Is that really so? I don't think it is. This is a child. He needs to be punished, yes, but he also needs our help. His life can be set right, he can be a worthy member of society. We have all been children, teenagers; we can all remember how uncertain we were about most things then, how little we knew and had experienced. How unreal death seemed, whether our own or that of someone we knew. If you're a teenager, nobody really dies. There is no such thing as death.

"You have found Jason Lee McGuire guilty of capital murder. Please find now that there is something redeemable in him. Please don't conclude that a life so young, so unformed, so desperately in need of guidance, must be snuffed out to avenge the tragic loss of Donald and Patrick McGuire. That would be the greatest tragedy of all. Thank you."

Edwards sat down, and Jason said, "Pretty good. You really laid it on them. Wonder if they'll buy it."

"The truth is," D'Orsino said, "that this young man is seventeen only if you count by the calendar. He may have been born seventeen years ago. But his crime and his evil are ageless. Two grisly murders—you've seen the photos.

His own father and brother—knifed to death while they slept. Systematically, brutally killed by this young man. He had no motive, no reason to do it. He isn't sorry. He's sat there for day after day as this horrible story has been retold and never batted an eye.

"Ladies and gentlemen of the jury, I don't relish standing here asking you to sentence this young man to death. That's not a job, frankly, that any of us can enjoy. But the fact is that under our laws that's what he deserves. We're not likely to see another crime like this in our lifetimes. Let us hope not. Let us do our duty under the law. Let us let other murderous thugs know that their hideous crimes will not be tolerated. Let us all try to make the world a little safer for people like you and me."

D'Orsino sat down.

"He was pretty good, too," Jason whispered to Edwards. "If I were on the jury I think I'd give me the chair."

Judge Schulz read the jury their instructions. They were to consider all mitigating evidence Jason had presented. They were also to consider all evidence that bore on the questions of whether the murder was especially heinous and whether it was premeditated. If the mitigating factors were equal to or outweighed the aggravating factors, said the judge, then they must sentence Jason Lee McGuire to prison for the rest of his life. If, on the other hand, they found that the aggravating factors outweighed those given in mitigation, then they must sentence him to death.

"You may begin your deliberations," said the judge. "Bailiff."

"It's been quite a while," Edwards said. He was sitting with Jason in a holding room near the courtroom and jury room. They were eating tuna salad sandwiches and drinking Pepsi.

"Yeah," said Jason. "You'd think it was a tough call."

"It is a tough call," he said. He paused to look at Jason over the rim of his soda. "I just can't see what got into you," he said. "You're a good kid. I just don't get it."

"Nobody's asking you to," Jason said.

"Your father didn't beat you up?"

"No, he didn't beat me up."

"Your brother?"

"No," he said.

"Bullshit," said Edwards. "They knocked hell out of you."

"Fuck off."

There was a knock on the door, and a guard stuck his head in.

"They're back," he said. Four and a half hours.

BATAVIA, Colum., Jan. 26 (AP)—Convicted teenage killer Jason Lee McGuire was sentenced today to die in the Columbia electric chair for murdering his father and brother last November. McGuire, 17, was convicted on Monday of capital murder in the two knifings. The jury needed less than an hour to find McGuire guilty of the crimes and just over four hours to sentence him to death.

"I think the jury's verdict was entirely proper and responsible," said District Attorney Joseph D'Orsino, who prosecuted the case against McGuire. "I'm just relieved it's over and that justice has been done."

McGuire stood impassively as the sentence was read. His attorney, Wendell Edwards of Batavia, shook his head slightly. Mrs. Key McGuire, the defendant's mother, bowed her head and appeared to pray as she heard her son sentenced to death. She had no comment.

The murders and the trial have rocked this peaceful farming town, which lies along the Batavia River in southwest Columbia, about 60 miles west of Monroe, the state capital. The last murder in Batavia took place in 1975, when a convenience-store clerk was shot to death in a bungled robbery attempt. The man convicted of that killing, Stephen Wesley of Leavitt, was electrocuted three years ago at the state prison in Warrensville. There has never before been a double murder in Batavia.

The case has also attracted statewide attention because of McGuire's youth. Civil-liberties groups have complained that it was unconstitutional to try a seventeen year old as an adult when doing so would subject him to the death penalty. They have launched a drive in the legislature to make it impossible for minors to be subject to the death penalty.

"We think the death sentence is just unconscionable," said Ted Zinman of the Monroe Coalition for Human Rights. "Executing seventeen year olds is not what America is all about."

McGuire's execution was set for March 23, but that date was automatically suspended while the state Court of Criminal Appeals considers the case. All death penalty judgments are automatically appealed to the high court.

6

On the road again. The Audi streaks along in overdrive, Manhattan Transfer in the cassette deck. "Tuxedo Junction." The weather clear and hot, and I'm grateful for the air-conditioning, which is on full blast. I'm grateful also to be getting out of Monroe for a day—two, actually, because I'm staying overnight. Caroline was not happy when I told her I had to go back to Warrensville.

"What for?" she said. "I thought you never had to go at all. Lots of those poor people never get to see their lawyers even once."

"There are major constitutional questions here," I said. "And there are major questions about the trial. About the murder. Edwards can't tell me anything. Jason's the only source."

"I thought he wouldn't talk to you."

"He will this time."

"You see this client more than you see the clients who

71

pay," she said rather cattily. Then she looked embarrassed because this is not a politically correct attitude and in Monroe that can cost you some dinner invitations. "You think about him more, too."

"I do not," I said.

But it's true: Jason is all I think about. In the middle of the day, when my desk is layered with briefs that have to be read, rewritten, when my phone is lighted up like a Christmas tree, associates asking questions, I find myself paging through the McGuire file, staring at the prison mug shots, the family shots, anything else I've been able to dig up. Mrs. McGuire sent me most of them, along with a note:

"Dear Mr. Delafield," it said. "Please help my boy. He doesn't deserve to die. I hope these are helpful." And she enclosed some photos, some of Jason's report cards, an essay he wrote from ninth-grade English on a Marx Brothers movie. "Duck Soup." Rufus T. Firefly and Freedonia. She didn't mention her return address, although the envelope was postmarked from someplace in Florida. I phoned Edwards about it.

"Yeah, she took off," he said. "Right after the kid got sent up. Couldn't stand Batavia anymore, that goddamned newspaper. She said she had to go someplace where nobody knew her or anything about her family. Wouldn't tell me where it was, either."

This whole thing makes no sense, I tell myself over and over. As though driving to this prison will make it all clear.

"Hey, boy."

The cell door creaks open, like a strange animal yawning: the sounds of dry skin against steel, of rancid breath rapidly being drawn, exhaled. It's still dark in the cell, and stifling. Too hot to sleep. The only light is cast by the naked yellow bulbs along the corridor. Jason sprawls nude on his little cot, arms crossed over his face. His hair is tangled and his skin flushed. The sounds of the key in the lock and the door opening awaken him instantly. It is too early for breakfast.

"OK."

"Man oh man," says another voice.

"Don't take too long," says the first voice.

"Take as long as I have to," says the second voice. "Been waitin' for this for a long long time."

"Hurry."

Jason feels a hand on his thigh. By instinct he pretends to be asleep, mutters something unintelligible and rolls toward the wall. Maybe this man will go away. Through the slits in his eyelids he sees a figure crouched at his feet. Then a hand stroking him, caressing. Rising panic.

"Bawk bawk," the man says softly, and keeps rubbing.

A hiss from outside the cell: "Hurry up!"

Jason bolts upright, as if suddenly awakened. Frighten the guy off. "Hey!" he says. "Who are you? What's going on?"

The guard stands nervously outside the cell, smoking a cigarette. He says nothing, makes no move.

"Don't you worry about the guard, pretty boy," says the man, whom Jason now recognizes as someone named Phillip. "He don't want his mother to get hurt."

Phillip is young and brawny and has a date with Gretchen for killing his own mother in an insurance scam. He exerts tremendous force in the weird, unofficial politics of the prison and the row; he is said to have many friends on the outside.

He pulls his shirt off. Then he kneels by Jason's side again and starts to suck him. Jason twists away, wanting to scream, but Phillip grabs his balls and squeezes them and says, "No use, pretty boy, you might as well go along for the ride."

Then he reaches up and grabs Jason by the hair on top of his head and kisses him hard on the lips. His breath smells like cigarettes and stale coffee.

"What do you want?" Jason says when Phillip pulls his mouth away.

"Your ass, you pretty little thing," says Phillip. "It's taken me long enough to get this far and you ain't gonna stop me now."

He stands up straight and with a single quick motion pulls his pants down to his ankles. Then they are off his feet. Then he is on top of Jason, hot and heavy, his erection pressed between them. His chest is hard and powerful, his arms strong. His skin smells like a man's. He begins to grind his hips against Jason.

"Ugh, ugh," he grunts, and Jason is afraid he is going to come right off. But Phillip rolls away after a moment.

"Likin' it a little bit, I see," Phillip says with a smelly grin. Jason says nothing. Phillip strokes Jason's cock, flicks the tip of it with his tongue. Meanwhile his hands are wandering between Jason's legs.

"Pretty boy," Phillip says, "there's something you can do for me."

He strokes his own cock for a moment while his fingers run to Jason's asshole. They tickle and probe and gradually he works one in. Jason lifts his hips a little. No point resisting, he tells himself. This guy is bigger than you are; he could tear you apart. Gently he strokes himself. The orange point of the guard's cigarette bobs anxiously this way and that.

"What are you doing in there, proposing?" he whispers desperately. "Get on with it."

"Don't rush me, man."

Phillip is on his knees now, lifting Jason's legs, putting them on his shoulders. He spits, rubs it around. Presses the head against the tight muscle and gives a little shove. He is surprisingly gentle. Slips right in.

"Ahhh," he says in a dizzy voice. He has waited a long time. "Ahh."

Pumping, pumping: Jason feels Phillip's balls slapping against his ass. In all the way, to the hilt, then back so that the head nearly emerges. The ecstatic violence of it. No thought interferes. Phillip breathes heavily, then starts to rasp.

"Pull it out," Jason whispers.

He works his hips in such a way that Phillip pops out, like a cork from a wine bottle, just as he begins to come. Jason milks. Phillip grunts as though he's having a heart attack. In a moment he slumps against the wall.

"Are you done?" the guard hisses. "Let's go! It's past five already."

Dawn is gathering in the east; the cell is filled with dark gray light. Jason lies motionless while Phillip pulls on his clothes.

"See you soon, pretty boy," he says as the guard hustles him back to his cell.

Jason runs his fingers through the splashes on his chest. He works it onto his palms like hand lotion and starts on himself. The fluid lathers up nicely, like soap. Just the right slipperiness. In a moment it is over.

The guard looks in on him as he passes. "I guess you'll need a shower today," he says. "Can't see your lawyer looking like that."

The cell smells like sex and his asshole burns. He feels oddly comforted. Then he vomits on the floor.

*　　*　　*

I should be less nervous than I was the last time I was here, but I am more. The town itself is creepy—dead under the hot July sun. My hotel is separated from the prison by most of Warrensville; it's made of cinderblocks and has an orange roof and a neon sign that says "Vacancy." It is the sort of hotel in which murders are committed. Or adultery. Child beatings. Drug deals. Rape tortures. Incest. No wonder they built a prison here.

I check in and go to my room and take off all my clothes and get into the shower. The water beats steadily on my back, and for the first time today I do not feel as though I'm losing my mind. I soap myself down and watch the bubbles as they swirl down the drain. No blood. It would be nice to stand here all day. While I'm shampooing my hair I take a piss and feel a little rush. Heart beating fast. Too fast.

Towel off, brush teeth, comb hair. Antiperspirant, cologne. Smell nice for the convicts. Then back into my suit, which seems tight even though I bought it only two months ago. Am I getting fat? I think I look good for thirty-three: trim, muscular, squash with one or the other of the new associates at least three times a week. I feel myself all over and don't feel any different. But when I do the collar it's hard to breathe. Must be the heat.

On my way to the prison I stop at Wendy's for a cheeseburger and Coke. Wolf it down as I drive down the two-lane road that leads to the gates, the guards, the walls, the watchtowers. Everything, everyone a glum gray. I can feel the food turning to acid as I drive.

He's waiting for me in the conference room. He's staring at his fingernails as I walk in. He looks paler than he did the last time I saw him; drawn, even. Prison does not agree. I say, "Hello, Jason," but he does not reply. Just a nod of the head.

I sit in the same chair I sat in the last time.

"How've you been?" I say. "Everything all right here?"

"What are you doing here, man?" he says without looking at me.

"I came to talk," I say, feeling my heart sink. He looks young and vulnerable, slouched against the table: he looks like a little boy who needs his mother to hug him. "I got a note from your mom."

"Yeah?" he says. He looks at me now, with his green eyes, and I feel the Wendy's gurgling around.

"Yeah," I say. "She wants you to know she's thinking about you. She wants me to help you."

"Did she say where she was?"

I hesitate. "No," I say. "But maybe she will soon."

"Maybe so," he says with a shrug.

"Listen," I say, "I've been working on your case quite a bit lately. The argument isn't too far off now."

"You don't need me," he says. "It's all just a bunch of lawyers talking to each other anyway. You must really like it here, man, huh? All the *guys*. Maybe they'll take you to the showers. Quite a show there sometimes."

"I don't know what you're talking about," I say. "I took a shower before I drove over here." Pause. "I came because there are some things we need to talk about."

"It's all there on paper, man," he says, folding his arms behind his head and stretching out his legs. These are the most vivid gestures I've ever seen him make. Animal gestures—completely natural, made without thinking. "Nothing more I can tell you."

"You can tell me why you did it," I say.

He smiles his wicked little smile, and I almost smile back. This time it's the smile of a charming rogue, of the handsome young rake who is frequently getting into trou-

ble, but not too seriously. Who's supremely confident of his
ability to con the principal.

"Doesn't make any difference why I did it," he says.
"Trial's over. Your only hope is to get me off with some of
your lawyer hocus-pocus."

It annoys me slightly that he knows even this much
about criminal law and the appellate process. "How do you
know?" I say.

"I could have been a lawyer," he says, "if I'd wanted to."

"Tell me why."

"Because I'm a cold-blooded killer," he says. "Just like
the papers say."

I do not need to know why he killed his father and
brother. I can make the arguments without knowing. But
the more I think about it—and I can't stop thinking about
it—the less comfortable I am at any time, about anything.

I do need to know.

"Look," I say, "I'm not asking you as your lawyer. I'm
asking as your friend."

"You're not my friend," he says.

"Yes I am," I say. "I want to help you. I care about what
happens to you. Why do you think I drive up here? For the
pleasures of Warrensville?"

"Nobody cares about me."

"Jason," I say, feeling vaguely unprofessional, "there's
something you have to understand about me. Law to me has
always meant people, not ideas. I can't just sit in a library
and grind out legal arguments. I have to know what I'm
fighting for. Who. You might think that's bullshit but it's
true."

"I think that's bullshit."

"So are you going to tell me?"

"Tell you what?"

"Why you did it."

"No," he says simply, and I can see I'm not going any further this afternoon.

"We're fine," Caroline says flatly. It is not a comforting voice. "We watched Cosby and ate dinner. How about you?"

"Fine," I say.

"Did you eat?"

"Sandy's Grill," I said. "I had the fried chicken dinner for $3.50."

"And how were things at the prison?" she asks. "Your little friend getting along OK?"

"He's not my friend," I say. "He's my client. I thought we'd cleared things up about that."

"Will you be back tomorrow for supper?"

"Yes," I say. She knows that I will. I promised.

I watch the TV for a while: "L.A. Law," the news. I can tell I'm not going to sleep well tonight. My room is on the ground floor, and there's a large window—without bars—that looks onto the parking lot. Which way is the prison?

Cramps wake me at about midnight from an uneasy doze. The air-conditioning is loud and not very cold and the neon light of the motel sign casts a ghostly blue glow across the plasterboard walls of my room. I go to the door and open it as far as the chain will allow. Hot, sultry air streams in. I must still be 75 degrees outside.

Can't stay here, can't sleep. Need air. I rummage through my overnight bag for my blue jeans and a T-shirt and tennis shoes. Then, leaving my wallet behind, I go out.

It's about a five-minute walk to the center of town. I trudge along the shoulder of the road, the gravel cracking beneath me, the occasional car whizzing by, toward Monroe or into the village and the prison beyond. Crickets sing in the trees and meadows on either side of me. There's a three-quarters moon and broken clouds sailing along on a gusty south wind. I feel less ill. I talk to myself a little, rehearse a phrase or two for Criminal Appeals, for Jason.

At length I reach Center Street, downtown, where there is an all-night grocery store. I buy a Diet 7-Up and take it across the street to the park, where I sit down on a bench. More cars down here, cruising restlessly along the street. The soda is sweet and cold and I can feel it running down my esophagus, spreading in my stomach.

A man about forty walks slowly by. He's dressed in jeans and a T-shirt and tennis shoes—an outfit that looks slightly ridiculous on him. He looks at me as he passes and I look back and he smiles and nods and I smile and say, "Hey." Another sip of soda. The man leaves the sidewalk and disappears into the park behind me.

There is something profoundly agreeable about country towns on warm summer nights. You know that people are around—good, gentle people—so you don't feel cut off, but the town itself smells and sounds of the country. You can see the stars as you can't in Monroe: they're bright, cold, clear, filling the sky like showers of motionless white sparks. I lean back on my bench and stare up at them.

Then he is back. I look up and he is passing in front of me again, smiling and nodding. This time I nod but do not say anything. He almost stops but not quite. I am out of soda so I suck on one of the ice cubes. He motions for me to follow him. I do.

The park occupies about three city blocks, and its center is dark and partly forested. I follow the man's white shirt as it moves along into a glade of trees. Hesitation. The prison—how far away?

"Psst."

There is the man, leaning against a tree. I can't see too

much other than his shirt, shoes and face: the white parts barely visible in the moonlight.

"Psst," he says again, and I think I see him motioning him closer. This is starting to seem crazy, but I take a step or two toward him. A step or two closer, to see what he is doing. He is doing something. I know what he is doing.

I stare a moment, then run away.

"I missed you," I say.

From the next room come Jessie's snores. She's wrapped up with Teddy, her teddie bear; the blankets are no doubt snarled and at least one of her three pillows has been thrown to the floor, more likely two. Jessie is an aggressive sleeper. Pity her husband-to-be, out there somewhere, safe in bed. No idea of the struggles that await. The battle of the pillows.

"We did all right," says Caroline.

"I don't understand why you're upset with me," I say softly. "I didn't do anything wrong. It was a business trip."

"I'm not mad," she says, half toward the wall.

Gently I reach for her, run my fingernails along her forearm. She groans with pleasure and squirms a little closer. But she does not turn toward me, and I cannot say I mind.

7

It is cool beneath the dome of the state capitol, even in the hot, lifeless days of August. Bryan stands in the middle of the rotunda, amid the stately columns of white Italian marble, and stares up at the mural painted on the inside of the dome. A tour group shuffles off somewhere behind him, their shoes clicking on the stone floor. He pays no attention. The mural depicts scenes in the development of Columbia: the Indians, the first settlers, agriculture, the building of Monroe.

The Court of Criminal Appeals sits on the second floor in a room hung with green velvet draperies, carpeted in evergreen, and painted with more scenes of Columbia's history. Not a large room, but imposing: heavy twin doors of solid oak open to a view of the raised bench, also of oak, behind which the five justices sit in leather chairs to hear cases. The bench is flanked by the flags of the United States and Columbia, each hanging from a brass staff seven feet high.

9:40. He listens to his heart beat, takes five deep breaths to slow it down. He always feels this way before he argues a case—anxious, slightly sick to his stomach; it is what makes him a good lawyer, he tells himself. He never takes things for granted. Each case is like his first.

Slowly he turns toward the wide stairs that lead to the second floor and to the oak doors, already swung open to accommodate the public and the press—among the latter, two reporters from the Batavia *Times-Courant*.

"Oyez, oyez!" calls the clerk. "The Court of Criminal Appeals of the State of Columbia is now in session. All those with business before this honorable court draw nigh."

The justices, cloaked in their black robes, file in slowly from the right side of the bench. They take their seats and wait, faces impassive, hands folded in front of them. The oak doors are shut. The room is full of reporters and onlookers. Chief Justice Richard Rovere, a kindly-looking, gray-haired man with unfashionable wire-rimmed spectacles, says, "We will now hear arguments in the case of McGuire against the state."

The state's case is being handled by Sandra Byers, an assistant attorney general in the criminal division. She was a year ahead of Bryan in law school and they had gone out a few times right after he started. Things never amounted to much. She is tall and intimidating, with a powerful, gravelly voice that resembles Lauren Bacall's.

Bryan and Sandra rise simultaneously, as if they'd been rehearsing.

"May it please the court, Bryan Delafield for appellant Jason Lee McGuire," Bryan says, and sits down without even glancing at Sandra, who looks most formidable in her dark blue suit and string of pearls.

"May it please the court," she says formally. "Sandra Byers, Assistant Attorney General, criminal division, for the state of Columbia."

"Thank you," says Chief Justice Rovere. "Mr. Delafield, please begin."

Bryan expects a difficult time of things, but he is far from pessimistic. Although the rest of the state might be clamoring to send every petty shoplifter to the chair, this is Monroe and the justices live here. True, they have been upholding death sentences at a steady rate in recent years, but they are not unreasonable, and he feels confident that they will respond to the very real errors he thinks the state committed in prosecuting Jason's case.

He moves to the lectern, sets down a yellow legal pad. On it he has scratched a few notes—reminders of the points he wants to make. Shards of phrases he wants to fit into his presentation. Over the last few weeks he has spent hours shut up alone in his study, staring at his research and the trial record, thinking out what it is he plans to say. What questions he is likely to be asked. He has buried himself in the law of the case. Now he knows how to win. That is what he was trained to do.

"May it please the court," he says. "I'd like to start by pointing out that the state's case rests largely on Jason McGuire's confession—a statement taken from him without a lawyer present, when the only other person in the interrogation room was a police officer. This is a clear violation of *Escobedo* and *Massiah*, and the trial court was therefore wrong to admit the statement at trial—"

"But Counsel," says Justice Betty Vandenberg, the only woman on the court, "there is nothing in the record to suggest that the statement was coerced, indeed that it was anything but voluntary. Didn't your client simply offer the confession?"

Bryan is ready for this question. "It may appear that way, Your Honor," he says, "but we mustn't forget that he was a seventeen-year-old boy all alone with a police officer in an interrogation room. We know that coercion can take subtle forms. And we know for a fact that the boy had no lawyer to advise him at that time."

"He didn't want one," says the Chief Justice.

"Your Honor," says Bryan, "I think there's a real question whether a seventeen-year-old boy is legally capable of waiving his right to counsel."

"He's old enough to commit murder," says Justice Ronald Bateman, the court's oldest, most conservative, and least agreeable member. Rumor is that even the other justices dislike him. But he is politician-shrewd, an ex-lieutenant governor, and he knows just the phrase to wreck defendants' cases.

"With all due respect, Your Honor," says Bryan, "that has no legal relevance."

"I think it's mighty relevant," says Justice Bateman. "You make much in your brief of the age of this defendant, but the truth is, Counsel, isn't it, that he's less a child than a young man?"

"He may physically be a young man," says Bryan, suppressing his unease at the course of the argument, "but psychologically, emotionally, he's very young. Not fully accountable for his actions."

"The trial court didn't agree with you," Justice Bateman points out in his rumbling voice. "Found him capable of standing trial as an adult and so certified him."

"We believe the trial court erred," Bryan says evenly.

"I'd like to get back to this confession," says the chief justice. "What, exactly, are you contending was a violation of *Escobedo?* The police advised your client of his right to remain silent and so forth. Are you saying that the mere fact that he was alone with a police officer in an interrogation room without a lawyer is a violation of *Escobedo?*"

"What we're saying," Bryan says, "is that nothing Mr. McGuire said between the time he was told a lawyer had been appointed for him—this was shortly after his arrest, after he had been given his rights—and the time the lawyer arrived ought to have been used against him. He was vulnerable during that time. He had no one to advise him. He was a scared, defenseless kid, Your Honors, and we don't know for certain that Detective Lipinsky didn't somehow coerce the confession."

Justice Bateman visibly sneers. The other justices look thoughtful. Bryan presses on with his other claims. When his thirty minutes are up, he sits down feeling drained. He did not anticipate all the questions, but he was ready for Bateman and feels pleased that he handled him so well. There is no way to win his vote, anyway, so the main thing was to keep one's poise, and stick to one's guns when dealing with him. Rovere was a bit of a surprise, but of course it was dangerous to try to guess how a justice was going to vote by gauging the tenor and substance of his questions.

Sandra Byers is talking about the rigorous adherence to process that had been followed in this case. She emphasizes that Lipinsky did not ask Jason a word about the murders, that he had simply been explaining police-station procedures when the boy burst out with his confession.

"How do we know that?" says Justice Vanderberg. "From Lipinsky's testimony?"

"Yes."

"But it was never corroborated. The defendant himself never testified."

"Your Honor," says Sandra, "the jury believed him. They listened to the witness and then decided. They were there. It is not our job to second-guess them."

Justice Vandenberg clearly seems troubled by this but does not press the point. Sandra, perhaps to placate her, emphasizes all the testimony that Jason felt no remorse, that he confessed gladly, on and on. Bryan pays little attention. The justices grill her about the propriety of the adult-certification process, whether the law was sound, if the state had good reasons for seeking certification against the boy. Her replies are solid, professorial. At length her half hour, ends, too, and they file out of the courtroom to go their separate ways.

I saw Sandra disappear down the long marble corridor toward the AG's office. She looked terrific and her long legs carried her past almost everyone else. For a moment I thought of asking her out to lunch but couldn't really think of a suitable pretext. Ever since law school we haven't had much to say to each other, have seldom seen each other, though Monroe's legal universe is cozy. Perhaps she felt as embarrassed as I did that things between us were so disappointing; and I think she never cared much for Caroline. In Sandra's world, women who sacrifice for their men are suspect.

I find, as I make my way down the broad stairs at the front of the capitol building, that my shirt is soaked with sweat, and my legs feel weak. I wobble toward my office, where there is a shower and a little cot so I can take a nap. Not all oral arguments are as debilitating as this one was, but of course the heat is terrible today.

To be honest, I wouldn't mind if they did execute Jason. He deserves it. At first the idea offended me: he is so young, so angelic looking in his way, and as a policy matter I can't see much good in putting child and teenage criminals to death. Sometimes, I'm sure—as in this case—they were fully aware of what they were doing and can be held to an adult standard of responsibility, but there will never be enough of them to make it seem anything but pointless and capricious. Or to bore the media. So when a kid gets it there will always be something loud on the front page and it will make our society look bad. In my view it's just not worth the embarrassment.

I don't want to lose; I don't mean that at all. I want to win. I expect to win, even if winning means I have saved the life of someone I dislike and think ought to be punished in the most severe way. I want to win the case, not for the client; I want my legal arguments to be vindicated. I happen to think they're right, besides.

It's odd to feel this way because I agreed to do the case more or less for emotional reasons. To save helpless people from undeserved fates, serve the aims of justice, protect the integrity of the process and the profession, etc. The classic Monrovian reasons. Now I find that I think of Jason's case as I think of any other case: as something I'm doing for myself.

Is that selfish, I wonder as I cut across the lawns of the Capitol Square toward my office. If it is, nobody can complain. I did a hell of a job this morning, after days upon days of research. The little prick should be grateful, but I know he won't be. He is the most bent-out-of-shape person I've ever met, of any age.

Maggie is waiting for me.

"There's a fresh towel on your chair," she says, "and I've set up the cot."

"Mrs. Pfingsten," I say, "you must have ESP."

"And if you'll tell me what you want for lunch I'll have someone bring it over."

"I think I may go home early today," I say. "Nothing crucial here, is there?"

"No."

"Any messages?"

"No," she says. "But I was out for a while. Shall I check the front desk?"

"They can wait."

Caroline generally calls to leave a congratulatory message on the mornings I'm in court, but she doesn't always, and I can't say I blame her for not saying anything about this case, of which she has never approved.

I pad in my stocking feet along the back corridors, down four flights of stairs, to the locker room of the health club in our building. Not good at all if the clients see a junior partner with sweat stains on his shirt and his hair all mussed up. The cold air of the office has given me a chill, and I sneeze so forcefully that one of my contact lenses momentarily drifts from its moorings atop my cornea.

The locker room is full of steam: one of the new associates has just come back from the gym downstairs and is in the shower. I quickly strip down and join him.

"Brett," I say.

"Hi, Mr. Delafield," Brett says.

"Bryan," I say. "Please. I'm not that old, am I?"

He laughs, the shampooey water running around his mouth. "I guess not," he says.

"Work out?" I ask.

"Yeah," he says. "Took an early lunch hour. Pete and I"—he's referring to another new associate "—play racquetball a couple times a week at this time. Easier to get a court."

He is finished with his hair now and has soaped down his entire body, so that he looks like a mummy.

I nod. Racquetball is déclassé, but no need to mention that now.

"How about you?" he asks.

"Just back from court," I say. "The kind with judges."

"I didn't know you were trying a case," he says as the water melts his white frosting.

"Criminal Appeals."

"Oh," he says. "That juvenile death-penalty thing. I read about it in the papers."

"It's gotten a lot of play."

"How'd it go?"

"OK, I thought," I say. "But who knows?"

"That's a weird case," he says. "My sister-in-law lives in Batavia—that's where the murders were, wasn't it? She sends me clippings from the paper. There's something weird going on there."

"What do you mean?" I say.

We step out of the shower and start to towel ourselves off.

"If just doesn't quite make sense to me," he says. "It's like they never establish a motive or anything but he still gets the death penalty. I'm not necessarily against the death penalty, you know, but I think we should know why somebody did something before we execute him for it."

"He admitted the whole thing," I say. "Unfortunately."

"It just doesn't seem quite fair to me," he says as he slips his white briefs on and buttons up his white shirt. "You know what I mean?"

"I know," I say.

It is only after he has knotted his Repp tie and gone back to his office that I realize I have forgotten to wash my hair.

State of Columbia
Court of Criminal Appeals

Jason Lee McGuire, Appellant
v.
The State.
No. 189-CR-516

The CHIEF JUSTICE delivered the opinion of the Court.

Appellant Jason Lee McGuire was convicted of two counts of capital murder and sentenced to death in the Circuit Court of Batavia County, Thomas P. Schulz, J. The case is before us on automatic appeal, 16 Crim. Code § 112(b)(2). We will affirm the judgment and sentence of the trial court.

I

At about 5:30 on the morning of November 3, appellant, then 17 years and three months of age, awoke and went to the kitchen of the Batavia home where he lived with his parents and two siblings—an older brother, Patrick, 18, and a younger sister, Colleen, 9. He armed himself with an 8-inch-long chef's knife with which he then methodically stabbed to death his father and brother. There were no witnesses to these murders.

Appellant's mother discovered the bodies shortly after seven that morning, when her efforts to wake the two men failed. She found appellant sitting in the kitchen eating toast, the bloody knife lying in the sink, and bloodstains on appellant's underclothes. There was no sign that the house had been broken into, or of the presence of an intruder.

Appellant was taken into custody after being advised of his right to remain silent and to be advised by a lawyer, *Miranda v. Arizona*, 384 U.S. 436 (1966). He then voluntarily confessed the crimes to Detective Joseph Lipinsky of the Batavia Police Department. No lawyer was present at the confession.

Because of his age and the viciousness of the crimes, appellant was certified to stand trial as an adult. The state timely served notice of its intent to seek the death penalty, 8 Crim. Code § 3(c)(1), on the ground that the murders were committed with "malice aforethought," 8 Crim. Code § 5(b)(4), and in a manner that was "especially shocking, outrageous, or vile," 8 Crim. Code § 5(b)(5).

At trial appellant objected to the state's introduction of his confession to Detective Lipinsky on the ground that it was obtained in violation of appellant's right to counsel. The objection was overruled.

Appellant also moved for a mistrial on the ground that his certification to stand trial as an adult denied him due process of law. This motion was denied.

The state's key witnesses were Detective Lipinsky, who related the confession and testified that appellant seemed pleased with what he had done, and Mrs. McGuire, appellant's mother. She testified to a number of the details of the morning of November 3.

Over the state's objection, appellant's young sister, Colleen McGuire, testified on behalf of her brother. Colleen McGuire testified that she often heard her father in her brothers' room and that violent noises came from the room while Mr. McGuire was in it. There was no direct evidence that Mr. McGuire beat either appellant or his brother.

Appellant did not take the stand in his own defense.

The jury found appellant guilty of two counts of capital murder. During the sentencing phase of the trial, the state introduced, over the defense's objection, photographs of the corpses as they were found in their beds by the authorities. The state also introduced appellant's alarm clock, which had been set for 5:20 on the morning of the murders.

The defense introduced appellant's good academic and attendance records at Batavia High School. Several witnesses testified to his good character. The defense also stressed appellant's youth as a mitigating factor.

The jury nevertheless recommended the death penalty on both counts because the murders had been committed with "malice aforethought." The judge accordingly sentenced McGuire to death. Execution of the sentence was automatically stayed pending the decision of this court.

II.

Appellant raises a number of issues before this court. We deal with each of them in turn.

A. VOLUNTARINESS OF CONFESSION

Appellant first contends that his confession—which was the linchpin of the state's case against him—was obtained in violation of *Escobedo v. Illinois*, 378 U.S. 478 (1964) and *Massiah v. United States*, 377 U.S. 201 (1964). He claims that once he had been taken into custody and requested a lawyer, all discussion of the case ought to have ceased, and that the confession was coerced by Detective Lipinsky's mere presence.

We recognize that in some cases there may be merit in the claim that the mere presence of a police officer may be sufficient to intimidate a suspect to confess, and that that possibility endangers the rights *Escobedo* and *Massiah* were designed to protect. But we cannot agree that such intimidation or coercion has occurred in this case.

It is true that Detective Lipinsky spoke to appellant after appellant had been told a lawyer had been appointed for him and was on his way to the police station. The detective's uncontradicted testimony, however, indicates that the subject of their conversation was not the crime itself but police station procedures. We think it clear that this was no violation of appellant's right to have a lawyer present during questioning, because there was no questioning.

Moreover, Lipinsky's uncontradicted testimony is that appellant offered his confession without any prompting and that after his confession he seemed pleased with himself. While there may be instances in which the mere presence of a police officer will constitute coercion, we are not persuaded that this is one of them. Lipinsky's testimony suggests that appellant was eager to confess and that he was indifferent to the presence of his lawyer. We are not prepared to say that appellant's statements, as reported by Lipinsky, amount to a waiver of appellant's right to have a lawyer present during questioning. But neither are we prepared to conclude that appellant's confession was coerced when the evidence appears overwhelmingly to the contrary.

We conclude that there was no violation either of *Escobedo* or *Massiah* or of appellant's Fifth and Sixth Amendments rights.

B. CERTIFICATION AS AN ADULT

Appellant claims that he was denied due process of law, as guaranteed him under the Fourteenth Amendment to the U.S. Constitution, when the trial court certified him to stand trial as an adult. We disagree.

It is well within the discretion of the trial court to decide whether a minor should stand trial as an adult. The trial court in this case carefully appraised the facts of the case and the relevant aspects of appellant's personality and maturity. The trial court is entitled to great discretion in these matters and this court will not interfere with its judgments unless the clear weight of the evidence suggests that an injustice has occurred. We find no evidence in this case that the trial court erred in certifying appellant to stand trial as an adult.

C. RIGHT TO COUNSEL

Appellant claims he was denied his Sixth Amendment right to competent counsel. He founds this claim on the failure of counsel to call appellant as a witness in his own defense. We conclude that the performance of appellant's counsel was well within the standards demanded by the Sixth Amendment. See *Strickland v. Washington,* 466 U.S. 668 (1984).

The mere fact that appellant did not take the stand to testify is not evidence of incompetent counsel. Indeed, appellant's trial counsel in this case seems to have represented his client with unusual vigor, objecting repeatedly to the introduction of state's evidence and to the certification of appellant to stand trial as an adult.

In light of that skillful advocacy, we find it impossible to believe that counsel's failure to call appellant to the stand was the result of ineptitude. We are persuaded that counsel was pursuing a reasonable strategy of which appellant's silence was a crucial component. The record will not support any other conclusion.

D. PHOTOGRAPHS OF THE CORPSES

The photographs of the dead bodies present a close question of evidence. We think that had they been introduced in the guilt phase of the trial they would clearly have been prejudicial, and we would be obliged to reverse the conviction and sentence. On the simple question of guilt or innocence, with the state already in possession of appellant's confession, the spectacle of the bloody corpses would have no bearing and would simply have posed an excessive risk of inflaming the jury.

That is not true in the sentencing phase, where the photos were in fact introduced. We agree with the state that the photos tended to show that the murders were "especially shocking, outrageous, or vile." And we conclude that the photos were not prejudicial, because the jury recommended the death sentence not on that basis but because the murders were committed with "malice aforethought."

E. Youth as a Mitigating Factor

Appellant argues that we must reverse the conviction and sentence because the trial court's instructions to the jury failed to emphasize that youth is a mitigating factor of "great weight" in capital sentencings. *Eddings v. Oklahoma*, 455 U.S. 104 (1982). We disagree that the trial court erred in this respect.

Columbia law entitles a capital defendant to introduce "any and all" mitigating evidence during the sentencing phase of his trial. 16 Crim. Code § 85(c). The statute does not specify mitigating factors. Nor does our case law suggest that a trial court commits reversible error when it fails to enumerate examples of mitigating factors.

In this case, while it is true that the trial judge did not say that appellant's youth was a mitigating factor of "great weight," he did tell the jury that they were to consider all possible evidence on appellant's behalf and noted that appellant was 17 years old at the time of the murders. Appellant's trial counsel repeatedly emphasized appellant's youth in his closing argument to the jury.

The trial court ought to have given a more explicit instruction and we hold prospectively that trial courts are bound, in appropriate circumstances, to instruct juries in capital-sentencing proceedings that youth is a mitigating factor of "great weight." But we cannot say on the facts of this case that the jury was unaware of appellant's youth or that they were not permitted to consider "any and all" evidence—including youth—in mitigation.

F. Eighth Amendment Issues

Appellant raises two Eighth Amendment issues. He argues that the execution of murderers who committed their crimes as juveniles is "cruel and unusual" punishment. He also contends that the electric chair is a "cruel and unusual" punishment. We find both claims meritless.

1. Execution of Juvenile Murderers. The Supreme Court has never held that the execution of a murderer who commits his capital crime before his eighteenth birthday offends the U.S. Constitution. See *Thompson v. Oklahoma,*—U.S.—,108 S.Ct. 2687 (1988).

This court has repeatedly held that the executiion of such persons does not violate any right guaranteed under the Columbia Constitution. At least twenty-five other states permit the execution of such persons. Execution of juvenile killers was permitted under the common law. Nothing in Anglo-American jurisprudence indicates that the execution of persons for crimes they commit as minors is impermissible. Accordingly we reject appellant's claim.

2. Use of the Electric Chair. Appellant claims that the electric chair is an unnecessarily grisly and painful method of carrying out the sentence of death. See *Glass v. Louisiana,* 53 U.S.L.W. 3773 (1985) (Brennan, J., dissenting from denial of certiorari).

We think appellant's Eighth Amendment claim must fail here simply on the ground that the electric chair is not an "unusual" method of punishment. The electric chair has been used to execute convicts for more than a century, and its constitutionality is well established. *In re Kemmler,* 136 U.S. 436 (1890).

Even if we agreed that appellant's arguments had some basis in fact, we think it the proper domain of the legislature —which is elected by the people and answerable to them—to determine how crimes shall be punished. Unless the legislature's choices plainly contravene some provision of the state or federal constitution, this court will not interfere.

III.

The conviction and sentence of death are affirmed. The case is remanded to the trial court with instructions to set a date for execution of the sentence not later than ninety days from the filing of this opinion.

It is so ordered.

Justice VANDENBERG, dissenting.

The Court holds today that murders committed by children too young to vote or buy beer are punishable by death. Because I believe that the Court's conclusion is fundamentally at odds with the Eighth Amendment's ban on cruel and unusual punishment, I dissent.

Even if I did not hold that view, however, I would reverse the sentence of death imposed in this case on the ground that the jury failed to consider relevant mitigating evidence: that of youth and of family violence.

I.

It is well settled that a punishment is "cruel and unusual" when it does not further any of the aims of criminal justice and becomes, instead, nothing more than "the purposeless and needless imposition of pain and suffering." *Coker v. Georgia*, 433 U.S. 584 (1977). It is equally well settled that the death penalty as applied to adults is a legitimate attempt by the state to deter crime and to express society's moral outrage at an especially brutal crime. See *Gregg v. Georgia*, 428 U.S. 153 (1976) (joint opinion of Stewart, Powell, and STEVENS, JJ.).

The Court, not surprisingly, makes short shrift of these policy questions, because there is little disagreement among child psychiatrists that death does not have the meaning for adolescents that it does for adults. Teenagers do not, for the most part, regard death—whether their own or someone else's—as real and are therefore not afraid of it. They are not afraid of the death penalty and will not be deterred by its prospect (which is remote for adults and even more improbable for them, in any event).

The Court also fails to recognize that adolescents lack the moral sense and responsibility to be held accountable for their actions in the same way adults are. Retribution is a function of moral culpability: we are entitled to express our outrage at someone who knows he is doing a grave wrong and does it anyway. See *Enmund v. Florida*, 458 U.S. 782 (1982). But a teenager—not yet an adult, not fully developed, not yet quite believing of the finality of death—surely cannot be deserving of this most severe of punishments, cannot have earned the eternal scorn of a society in which he is not yet entitled to play a full part.

II.

An even more troubling matter is the apparent failure of the judge in this case adequately to instruct the jury on mitigating factors. The Court holds that in future proceedings a judge's failure to instruct on youth as a mitigating factor will be reversible error. But it concludes in this case that the lack of adequate instruction did not taint the proceedings. It also completely sidesteps the trial judge's failure to instruct the jury, despite defense counsel's request, that evidence of family violence could support a mitigating factor of "diminished capacity" or self-defense.

There is doubt in my mind that these murders were unprovoked—enough doubt to persuade me that justice will not be served by the execution of this young defendant. The combination of defendant's youth and the possibility of his having been the victim of family violence is, to me, weighty enough for the Court to conclude as a matter of law that the jury was improperly instructed and that the case should be remanded for resentencing.

I dissent.

PART II
FAMILIES

8

The week before Christmas we decide to get Jessie a puppy. I was opposed at first, on the ground that she was only four and hardly in a position to assume much responsibility for a pet, but Caroline insisted that at the very least we ought to visit the SPCA and see what they had.

"It can't hurt to look," she said.

"I suppose not," I said.

Jessie was disappointed when an afternoon's exhaustive search of the Monroe Zoo turned up no signs of pandas. She shook her little fist angrily at us and then burst into tears and then became fascinated by a pair of snow leopard kittens playing with each other in their mother's cage.

"Kitties!" she said, clapping her little pink mittens together, "kitties!"

"Very good, honey," Caroline said, holding her up so she could see more easily into the cage.

I felt certain that a demand for a pair of snow leopard kittens wasn't far off, but the attractions of the animals, one after the other, kept us all occupied until it was time to go. Even a hostile goose that reached out its long neck to nip Jessie's leg was more a joke than a threat.

"Maybe we can see if they have kittens, too," Caroline says.

"I'd rather have a dog," I say. "I thought you said we're just looking."

"We are."

The SPCA building is little more than a large shack on the unchic east side of town. Just down the road is the airport and a big ball-bearing plant. You would think that Monroe would put its dog pound in a grand building in some ritzy neighborhood. But perhaps the dogs bark, or smell bad.

They do. We walk into the dingy lobby and are greeted by a trumpet of yelps and the sharp stench of piss. A blond woman, forty or so, tired but kindly looking, is seated at a desk filling out some forms for a middle-aged chap who holds a squirming puppy in his arms. The puppy is trying to lick his face.

"Any other pets at home, Mr. Armstrong?"

"No," says the man. "She'll be an only child."

"She's had all her shots," says the woman. "But you do have to have her spayed when she's six months. That's our rule. Here's a list of local vets who'll give you a 50 percent discount."

OK, nods Mr. Armstrong. Caroline motions toward the cages that lie beyond a big green door, and the woman nods yes. She leads; I follow.

We find ourselves walking slowly down a concrete aisle, steel cages on either side, from behind which we are regarded. Barks. Whines. Tails wagging fiercely. Squeals of delight as Caroline stoops to pet a young male, part shepherd, part labrador. He licks her hand through the bars as though it were coated with sugar.

"You've made a friend," I say.

"Adorable."

I find myself talking to what looks a good deal like a purebred Newfoundland, only smaller. Her black fur is long and glossy, her brown eyes slightly elongated, Asian. Her legs are too short for a real Newfoundland, however, and her skull is too flat and wide. Retriever blood in her somewhere. She makes a low growl of pleasure as I stroke her head as best I can with fingers stuck through the bars.

Some of the dogs lie there, inert and uninterested in us or anything else. Only their eyes move, following us as we troop down the concrete, peering into each cage to investigate each inhabitant, each sound.

Caroline worries about the less attractive and less peppy dogs.

"What do you think happens to them if nobody wants them?" she asks.

"I'm sure somebody wants them," I say. We both know this isn't true. We both know what happens. Probably not too far from where we're standing. Most eerie, the dogs seem to know, too. Their pleas for freedom are almost more than I can bear.

We turn a corner, pass more occupied cages, and find ourselves outside, making our way through the snow and cold toward a large cage, seven feet high, perhaps ten yards square, in which three German shepherd pups are playing with each other. At the far end of the cage is a little house to shelter them from the elements. As we approach they race up to the bars, one of them piling on top of the other two for an improved view. They wag their tails fiercely and bark the way all puppies do: Play with us. Get us out of here. One of them has been eating snow and has a little white beard at the bottom of his mouth.

"Oh," Caroline says helplessly, and I know she is wondering if the house is big enough to accommodate three adorable German shepherd pups that, in a matter of months, will be large, active dogs. It is a big house, but not that big. We would need a farm to keep these dogs, I am thinking but do not say.

"These look like German shepherds," I say to the boy who has come out to feed them. "Purebred?"

"Yep," he says. "Eight weeks old. Came in a few days ago. Family couldn't keep the whole litter."

"Of course, they're puppies," says Caroline. "I'm sure you have no trouble placing puppies. They're so cute."

"We do the best we can, ma'am," says the boy succinctly. He does not add that a lot of people don't want puppies, don't want to have to train them, put up with their chewing and rough play and messes.

She looks at me unhappily and squats down to the pups. They scramble to lick her hand; eventually their little pyramid collapses and they fall to wrestling and nipping each other. She watches them from her squat.

"Jessie would love them," she says.

"They're not pandas," I say. "It's cold. Let's go back in." The dogs by this time are aware that lunch has arrived and have scampered to the other side of the cage to greet the boy with the food. We thank him and head back for the main building.

"What do you think?" she says.

"The shepherd puppies?"

"Yes."

"Irresistible," I say. "But we can't possibly handle them all. Maybe not even one."

"I don't know," she says, but she knows. "It would be a pity to split them up. They're family. They're all they've got."

"Somebody'll want them for sure," I say, taking her hand, hoping I'm right, that those adorable little babies will avoid the gas chamber or the lethal injection or however it's done.

In a large room inside we find another group of puppies frolicking in an enclosure lined with shredded paper. Stacked on the walls around are cages full of kittens, tiny handfuls of fluff. Cotton balls with eyes and tails. The kittens, watching the antics of the young dogs, are absolutely still, though one or two are asleep. I stick a finger in one of their cages and the kitten, a soft gray bundle with dark gray eyes, sniffs it and paws at it. Caroline has reached into the puppy cage, meanwhile, to pet a tiny golden retriever. The dog rolls on its back and allows her to stroke his belly; as she does so he tries to get her hand in his mouth. She rocks him back and forth, laughing: they are both laughing. The kitten is trying with no success to get her claws through my fingernail.

"Well," I say, "they certainly are cute."

"They certainly are."

"It's a good thing we didn't bring Jessie," I say, "or there's no way we'd get out of here without one of these guys."

"That's what we came for, remember?" she says.

"I thought we came to look."

"You can't just look, Bryan," she says. "They need us. Look at them."

"We can't take them all," I say. But we are not going to get out of here without the golden puppy, I see.

"That kitten likes you," she says.

"I like her," I say.

"They could play with each other," she says.

"Dogs and cats," I say. Don't they always fight?

"If you raise them together they get along," she says. How she knows this I am not sure. But it seems to make sense—enough sense, at any rate, that we are soon at the

front desk making arrangements for our new golden
retriever and kitten.

Jessie is lying on the floor of the living room laughing
helplessly because Morton Kondracke is licking her face.
Dawn regards the festivities with caution from the top of
the piano. Morton Kondracke: that was Caroline's idea.
She's a "McLaughlin Group" groupie. The hair color is
wrong but the facial expressions are amusingly similar.
All we need is a pair of glasses and a preppie tie and a
blue blazer; Msgr. McLaughlin would never know the
difference.

"He sort of looks like him, don't you think?" she said as
we drove home from the kennel.

"He looks like a golden retriever puppy," I said. "Anyway we can call him Connie and seem like normal dog
owners."

"Mor-ton," she said in her most sonorous tone. "He'll
like that."

"I hope he doesn't want to argue with all the other
animals."

The first meeting between Dawn and Morton Kondracke was not a success. He wanted to play; she hissed at
him and bared her claws and leapt to the top of a chair. In
his excitement he soiled the kitchen floor, and in the frenzy
of our cleanup she bounded away toward the living room.
Morton Kondracke followed. It was some time before order
was restored. Jessie found the whole business a great pleasure. She laughed and clapped her hands and screamed
when Dawn jumped into her lap.

Dawn was my idea. That's her coloring, after all, and I
wanted her to grow up with some dignity. Jeane Kirk-

patrick: out of the question. Jessie could never pronounce that.

"You named the dog," I said. "I get the cat."

It is a brilliant Christmas Eve morning. The sunlight glints off a layer of fresh, powdery snow, and the air is cold and clear. Scents of pine trees and wood smoke; the kids down the block making angels on the white blanket. The whole house is filled with light. Later on, Caroline's and my parents will join us for Christmas Eve dinner; everybody will be up again for Christmas Day. Not to mention unannounced visits of friends. In the meanwhile, we have the day to ourselves.

"I'm going to get the mail," I say. Morton Kondracke bounds after me as I head toward the front door, and I lift him into my arms to carry him outside. Perhaps he will see to some business. Jessie whines about his defection, but Caroline points out that Dawn is still inside, atop the piano. With the puppy removed the kitten relaxes noticeably.

"Don't run off, Mort," I say, as the tiny golden thing bolts down the sidewalk ahead of me. He stops abruptly, squats and pees. I pull the mail out of the box. It's cold and I shiver, but it's probably worth it to give the little nipper more time.

Nothing. "Mort," I say. "Come on. Inside. Come on."

Morton is making his way through the two-foot-deep snow like a tiny porpoise—up and down, up and down. His legs are too short to keep the rest of him above the snow line, so each step is a leap. He loves it and ignores my pleas. Only when I walk determinedly toward the door does he follow. But he will not cross the threshold, and I must carry him in.

*   *   *

"What's wrong?" Caroline says. She's trimming the fat from the roast. Baked potatoes, broccoli with cheese sauce, cranberry sauce, fresh bread, river-bottom fudge pie: this is the beginning of a Christmas Eve dinner to be reckoned with. "You look worried."

"Not at all," I say.

"Something in the mail?" she says. "Not the electric bill again so soon?"

"No," I say.

It is a card from Florida. I don't know anyone in Florida. A simple Christmas card with a decorated evergreen tree on the cover. "Merry Christmas," says the printing inside. Handwritten: "Dear Mr. Delafield, I want to thank you for doing so much for my boy. I know you did as well as you could and I'm glad that he had a good lawyer. I wish he would tell somebody the truth. Maybe someday he will, and I hope it's to you. Have a good new year. Sincerely, Kay McGuire."

I show the card to Caroline.

"Look at this," I say.

She reads the card and makes a weary face. "Poor lady," she says. "She must be lonely. Christmas in Florida, nobody there for her."

"What does she mean?" I say aloud, though not really to Caroline. "What does she mean about telling the truth?"

"I don't know," Caroline says. "You know how we mothers are. Probably that we don't really understand her son. Who knows? Probably nothing."

"I don't think nothing," I say.

The fire has burned low and Jessie is in bed, gone to sleep and dreaming of Santa and reindeer, Rudolph and red nose, the sleigh piled high with gifts as it glides among the stars. Ho ho ho. My parents and I are sitting in the living room trying to stay awake after several bottles of good red Bordeaux. Most of Caroline's stupendous meal has been eaten, and there is a strong feeling of bloat. Morton Kondracke is lying on his side, feet to the fire; Dawn is asleep in my mother's lap.

"I don't like cats," she says, "because they kill birds and I love birds. But this one seems very nice."

"Cats have to eat, too," says my father. "They're not murderers."

Caroline has gone downtairs to bring the presents for Jessie's stocking out of hiding. We explained to her days ago that Santa probably wouldn't be bringing her anything major after she'd already gotten the kitten and puppy, but we eventually decide that Mort and Dawn are at least as much for us as for her, and in any event it's no fun for a four year old to wake up on Christmas morning and find no presents waiting. Children remember those things.

Outside it is snowing again, lightly. Snowing all over the state. Snowing in Batavia. In Warrensville. Caroline's parents went home an hour ago. They plan to get up early in the morning and go cross-crountry skiing.

"You couldn't pay me to do that," says my father.

"These are the times I love most," says my mother, stroking Dawn. "The family together by the fire on a snowy winter night."

"That's because you don't have to worry about the drive home," says my father. "Well," he says to me, "I'm sorry you lost that death-penalty thing. With that kid. Caroline tells us he's young."

My parents are staunch New Dealers, weaned on the gospel of FDR. In recent years they've updated their liberalism to include an opposition to capital punishment.

"He is," I say. "But I'm not too sorry."

"We're proud of you that you took the case," says my mother. "That you stood up for something you believed in."

"I took the case," I said carefully, "because I think we owe it to ourselves to make sure the system is running with all its parts in place. People have got to have lawyers."

"I'm sure he's a nice boy, really," my mother says. "There must have been something terribly wrong there."

"He's not nice at all," I say. "I wouldn't feel all that sorry for him if I were you. I've met him and believe me it was no fun."

Caroline appears bearing the gifts: toothbrushes, a box of homemade fudge, a nice winter bonnet for the stocking; a large stuffed panda doll, which she sets down under the tree. Morton Kondracke comes to life at the sight and sniffs the panda, hoping perhaps it will want to play. But his overtures are stonily rebuffed and he returns to the hearth to lie down.

"Caroline," says my mother, "we wondered what had happened to you."

"I wanted to get it all in one trip," she says as she arranges the loot in the stocking and hangs it from the mantel.

"We should go," my father says. "Boy can I feel the wine."

"You're not drunk, are you?" says my mother. "Because if you are, I'll drive."

"I'm not drunk," he says, "just tired."

We help them with their coats, walk them to their car, give them little hugs.

"Be careful," we say.

"See you tomorrow," they say, and get in and drive off. We hurry back into the house, shivering. Morton Kondracke is retired to his cage in the kitchen for the rest of the night; Dawn is allowed to prowl a spare bedroom with nothing valuable at hand for clawing.

"It's been a perfect evening," she says when we're in bed, in each other's arms.

"We're very lucky."

"Yes."

"I love you," she says.

"I love you, too."

She wants to make love and it takes me a while to get it up. Not really in the mood tonight but. Eventually we fuck, she with great enthusiasm. She licks my nipples and claws my butt and pounds herself against me so that I feel like I'm the one who's getting it instead of her. When she comes she bites my earlobes. I nearly cry out from the pain but manage not to. Her orgasm is one of those sweaty, heaving, grunting ones—the kind that put you right to sleep. She goes right to sleep. I do not come, but I go right to sleep anyway.

9

Jason sat squat-legged on the grass, watching the ants march in a straight line from a bit of rotted apple to their hill. When Patrick wasn't looking he took his can of Coke and poured it on the anthill. The sand foamed up nicely. The tiny creatures at first scattered in panic, but after a moment order began to be restored and damage to the hill repaired. Jason poured more of Patrick's soda on them.

"Hey," Patrick said, his attention wandering from the game. "Mom! Look what he's doing! That's my Coke, you little queer!"

"Patrick," said Kay McGuire. "That's not a nice thing to call your brother. Jason, what have you been doing?"

Jason pouted in silence. Patrick glowered at him. Although there was only a year's difference in the brothers' ages, Patrick seemed much older; perhaps because he had already completed second grade and Jason was only a year out of kindergarten. Or perhaps for other reasons.

"Boys, no more playing with the soda. Now I want you both to pay attention to the game. Look who's batting!"

Over on the field big Don McGuire strode to the plate, wielding his bat like a bit of kindling. Mighty Casey. He dug himself into the batter's box with great assurance and awaited the first pitch. One out, a runner at second; a chance to knock in a run.

"Park it, Dad!" screamed Patrick. Kay clapped loudly. The pitcher blooped the ball toward the plate and Don took a mighty swing. The ball skidded harmlessly toward the third baseman. He held the runner at second and easily threw Don out at first.

"What happened?" Jason asked.

"Tapper," said Patrick.

"Maybe next time," said Kay. "Boys, have you eaten your potato salad?"

"I hate it," Patrick said. "Dad never makes me eat it. He doesn't like it, either. What do you make it for?"

"Because it's good for you," she said. "Jason?"

"I liked it," he said.

"Jason, you may have dessert," she said. "Patrick, first finish your salad."

Now it was his turn to sulk. But not for long. Don McGuire came loping over from his team's bench, waving to his sons and calling to his wife for a piece of that chocolate cake.

"Great hit, Dad," Patrick said. "Could have been a double."

"Maybe next time," he said. "You just watch. The guy's throwing junk. These two behaving?" he said to Kay.

"Very nicely," she said. "We're just getting ready for some cake. There's a piece for you."

"Hit me," said Don McGuire. "I'm starved."

Kay handed out the pieces of cake, reserving only Patrick's.

"None for Patrick?" asked Don.

"He hasn't finished his supper yet," said Kay.

"Potato salad," said Patrick.

"Hate that stuff," Don said. "Did you eat your hotdogs?"

Yes.

"Corn on the cob?"

Yes.

"Drink your Coke?"

What Jason didn't pour down the anthill, yes.

"Hell, Kay, the boy's eaten practically all his supper. Let him have the cake."

"He hasn't finished the potato salad," Kay said stubbornly. "I told him he had to."

"Let him have the cake," Don McGuire said, and Kay quietly served Patrick his piece of cake.

"Mmmm-mmm," said Don. "Great stuff. Gang, I've got to get back. Still two innings to go. After the game we'll get root beers, how's that?"

"All right," Patrick said.

Don McGuire played softball every Tuesday night, from June through August, weather permitting, with a team from the construction company. Kay often took the boys to watch. Patrick was a budding athlete and spent a lot of time with his father practicing his skills—throwing, hitting, fielding, passing the football, shooting baskets. He was only eight and small, but scrappy and surprisingly adept.

"Attaboy," Don would say to him. "You're getting the hang of it."

Patrick and Jason played their own games but often got kicked outside for, as either Kay or Don would put it, "roughhousing." Sometimes Patrick would try to instruct Jason in the techniques of organized sport, but his own skills weren't yet that good and Jason apparently had little talent and less interest. Together they stuck to the games they invented, hiding among the trees or chasing after the soccer ball. But when their father appeared, Patrick dropped these juvenile amusements in favor of real sports. Jason disappeared.

"Well, ready to go?" Don's voice boomed across the field. It was almost dark now, and the crickets were singing in the bushes behind the backstop. They packed up their things and headed for the car.

"Did you win, Dad?" Patrick asked.

"Almost," said Don. "Maybe next time."

"I watched the whole game," Patrick said. "Jason didn't."

"Did so," said Jason.

"Should I drive?" Kay asked. "You look tired."

"Hell no. I'm fine," said Don.

At the A&W, Don and Kay ordered root beers, while Patrick and Jason had root beer floats.

"Don't spill back there, boys," Kay warned.

"Ah, hell," Don said. "They're all right."

"I think you're a queer," Patrick said that night, after they'd gone to bed. The room was faintly lit by the moon, and through the open windows came the sound of crickets. It was a hot summer night—hard to fall asleep. The air damp and heavy, clinging to their skin.

"I am not," Jason said. He did not know what a queer was, did not want to know.

"You are," Patrick said. "Wait till you get to second grade. You'll hate it. Everyone's going to beat you up and call you a queer."

"They are not."

"Are too."

"Are not."

"Wait and see, queer."

A moment's silence. Patrick had not planned his offensive past this point, and he was trying to think of a way to proceed with his advantage.

Then Jason said, "You're a queer, too."

"What'd you say, queer?"

"I said, you're a queer too."

"I am not a queer," Patrick said.

"If I am, you are," Jason said. "We're brothers."

"I am not a queer," Patrick said, and he got out of bed and came over to Jason's bed and started to beat him over the head with a pillow. "Take it back," he hissed. "Take it back."

"Shit on you," Jason said, and then Patrick pulled his hair and he started to cry. "Stop it," he screamed, "stop it!"

"Queer."

Patrick let go and got back into his bed. Jason ran from the room crying; burst into his parents' room without a knock. They were lying there motionless, back to back with a nice space between them. He crawled into the space and sobbed quietly.

"What's wrong?" Kay murmured. "Is that you, Jason?"

Sniffles.

"Is everything all right?"

"I had a scary dream," Jason said.

"Oh, honey," she said, cradling his head. "It's all right. It's only a dream. You rest here a minute and go back to bed. Everything will be fine."

Don didn't say anything, but he rolled onto his back and let Jason crawl under his arm. After a while they all drifted off to sleep.

*   *   *

The McGuires' was an all-American story. Kindergarten classmates, high-school sweethearts, King and Queen of Batavia High's senior prom (he the ace pitcher of the baseball team, she the head of the pom-pom squad), their pictures all over the senior yearbook. Don looking splendid in his rental tux. Kay luminous in white evening gown, holding a bouquet of roses.

Then the big church wedding and the nice little starter house; the honeymoon at a resort up north, where things did not go terribly well the first night but slowly got better. Back home to start life. Don had a good construction job building highways and warehouses; Kay at home cooking, cleaning, sewing, taking care of the first of what no one doubted would be a healthy count of children.

If she had been asked on the morning of her wedding why she was marrying Don, she would have said, slightly cross-eyed, mouth a little slack from genuine surprise, "Because I love him, of course."

Of course. She did love him and he loved her. Always had. They were brought up to love each other. To marry each other and have a family and live happily ever after. The American dream. This was the way it was supposed to be. This is what love was. No one asked, anyway. They did not ask themselves. No need.

Their world was Batavia. The rest of it was out there, yes, somewhere beyond the river and the hills, beyond the eccentrics in Monroe, making their goofy laws; but the world left them alone. They might have been living in a country village in medieval England, so isolated were they from the world outside. Television was a link to that world, as were the occasional trips to larger cities, but these contacts always struck the McGuires as unreal. Batavia was what was real. Where they had grown up. What they believed and lived.

Don settled smoothly into his life as a construction worker, gradually working his way up the line of authority, so that by the time he was twenty-five he was a subforeman and doing as much supervising as heavy labor. He liked both: liked the muscles and brawn that grew from all the lifting and shoveling; liked being in charge of a group of men.

Kay learned how to make chicken Kiev and beef Wellington, and periodically they entertained one or the other set of their parents with one of these newly mastered recipes.

The first little boy, Patrick, was a joy. Strawberry blond, strong, high-spirited, he was forever making demands on his parents and they were happy to satisfy them. On Sunday afternoons the boy sat for hours in his father's lap, watching the football games, listening to explanations of what was happening. Don rubbed Patrick's back; Patrick rubbed Don's scalp. They raked leaves together, shoveled snow together: a touching sight, the husky, six-foot-tall young man and his tiny son, both wielding their shovels. Patrick sometimes undid Don's good labors, returning the snow or leaves to an area just cleared, but no matter.

Jason, born a year later and named after Don's grandfather, was so quiet that for the first few days he was home they weren't sure he was well. He almost never cried, even when hungry or wet; the only noise he made was a whimper, a tiny bleat that barely issued through lips wrapped around a thumb.

They slept in the same room together, the boys. No real problems. Patrick was inclined to be a bully, and Jason would have his little revenges: shitting on the floor beside Patrick's bed, for instance, or taking his clothes out of the dresser and scattering them about the room. Hiding his toy ships. Minor incidents: testament to the vigor of boys and colorful additions to family lore. Jason idolized Patrick nonetheless, wanted to be just like him. Same clothes, same food, toys, books. Kay took pictures and marked the date and dramatis personae on the back of each one.

Don found Jason a mystery. Patrick was a robust child, open and eager, quick to get angry or to laugh; Jason was quiet, secretive, difficult to read. Almost instinctively Don did not pursue with his younger son the athletic agenda Patrick had learned so well. Jason was big and strong, too, and fair and handsome—but with no taste for male camaraderie. There was the occasional snowball fight, the infrequent game of catch, but never Don and Jason alone. Patrick was always there; Jason always the third party and fifth wheel, never enthusiastic.

At school the brothers went their separate ways, but happily. Groups of guys. Girls were suspect, to be dealt with only when necessary. Patrick liked to play kick ball and the other team games; Jason favored the jungle gym. Sometimes their paths crossed, but not often. Both made friends, all of whom seemed very nice to Kay when they showed up after school to play or eat her freshly baked chocolate chip cookies. Kay was relieved that Jason was moving on his own, not so dependent on Patrick. Becoming a little person.

"What's sperb?" Jason asked Patrick one night, when they were lying there in the dark. He had noticed some changes in his brother's body: hair under the arms; a voice that sounded as though he had a cold all the time. He wondered if Patrick were sick, dying; why weren't they telling him? A disease? Would he get it too?

Girls. Half the ninth grade seemed to be calling for

Patrick—the guys wanting to go out and find chicks, the
chicks giggling briefly on the line before hanging up.
There were the group get-togethers at McDonald's, after
football games; there was the occasional movie. Patrick hid
Playboys underneath his mattress. Obsessive reflections on
the driver's license.

"You mean sperm," he said. He laughed. "You don't
know, do you?"

"I think I do," Jason said.

"No, you don't."

"What is it?"

"I'll show you," Patrick said.

"You have some?"

"Sure do."

He switched on his bedside light and he was lying on
his back naked, stroking himself. His dick looked absolutely colossal to Jason in the half shadows—like a pillar.
Terrifying.

"What are you going?" Jason said in an urgent whisper. He was unable to take his eyes from the sight, and he
felt himself swelling, growing hot. His body was changing,
too—hair in awkward places, erections at awkward times,
amazingly persistent, nothing he could do about them—
but he hadn't told anyone and he hoped Patrick hadn't
noticed. Or his teachers. Science was the worst. Algebra
not far behind.

"Showing you," he said in a funny, strained voice. He
grunted a little and his hand moved faster—"Watch"—and
he arched his back and fluid shot out. Not pee.

"Oh," he said, and sagged back against the pillows.
"See?"

Like a cat Jason crept out from between his sheets to
examine this new, unknown substance. He looked at
Patrick's stomach, the viscous, milky fluid.

"Can I touch?" he said.

Patrick nodded.

Jason ran a finger through the sperm. Smelled it. Like fresh, damp dirt. What did it taste like? Patrick watched proudly.

"How did you learn how to do that?"

Patrick laughed and turned off the light. "I just figured it out," he said. "Lucky for you you've got an older brother."

"I guess," Jason said, not knowing what else to say. He crawled back into his own bed and lay there straining against his underwear. Soon Patrick began to snore. Jason thought about getting out of bed again, going over to his brother, touching his belly, but he didn't. Instead he pulled his own underwear down halfway and started to rub himself the way Patrick had done. He did this for a while, but nothing happened except that it started to feel raw. He gave up and went to sleep.

New Year's Eve. The last guest five minutes out the door, down the icy walk, into the car, key in the ignition, numb starter motor grinding. Battery almost gone. Ten below zero.

Kay in the kitchen, rinsing glasses, cleaning out ashtrays, putting crackers back into boxes, wrapping up uneaten cheese. Tears gathered at the corners of her eyes.

Don drunk on the sofa. A can of beer dangling from his unsteady hand. Eyes glazed red; an unpleasant smile on his face. Sprawled.

"God," he says out loud. "What a great party." He farts into the sofa cushions. A burp. Sounds of industry from the kitchen. Slowly he gets to his feet to investigate. Who would be working in the kitchen at this hour?

It's Kay. He recognizes her, says "Hey babe."

"Don't call me babe," she says in a cutting voice.

"Hey," he says. "I'll call you anything I want. Babe."

She scrubs and empties and cleans.

"Why are you doing all this now?" he says. "Let's go to bed. Do it in the morning."

She says nothing. He reaches out and puts his arms around her. She makes a forceful move toward the sink and dislodges one of his arms.

"Hey," he says, very softly.

"I've got work to do," she says. "And you're drunk."

"I sure am."

"You made a fool out of yourself tonight. Out of both of us."

"Whatever you say."

"Carrying on with your fat jock friends who don't amount to a hill of beans."

"Bitch," he says.

"You sleep in the extra bedroom tonight," she says. "It's closer to the bathroom. In case you get sick."

He wants to hit her but doesn't. Instead he lumbers off to the guest room where, fully clothed, he falls into black oblivion.

"I can't," Jason says. "It hurts."

"You need something slippery."

"Like what?"

"Spit," he says. "Or something."

"No spit tonight."

"Here."

Patrick reaches under his bed, produces a bottle of hand lotion. "Try this." He flips the bottle to Jason.

Jason gets it all over his hand and starts to pump.

Much better. An incredible feeling. It slips easily through his fist; hips start to work on their own. Fire running from his groin. Pulsing. His breaths are deep. Heart beating wildly. All over his chest and belly. Less than a minute.

"Yeah," says Patrick. "Now you've got it." He is done a moment later. It is the first time Jason has ever felt close to his brother.

They clean up with toilet paper Patrick has brought from the bathroom and collapse into sleep. They do not hear their father staggering along the corridor toward the guest room. They do not hear their mother, either—her weary, bitter trudges toward an empty bed.

10

I can understand how marriages collapse. Or rot or whatever. Just wear out. I mean, look at the McGuires. They married young, with no education. They didn't know about the world, who they were, what they wanted. They just went right ahead and did what they were expected to.

Of course they got bored. The kids, the responsibility, the days of toil stretching endlessly before them. No hope, really. No plan; no end in sight or imagination. Life gone stale, like week-old bread. I know how they must have felt—not that I'm in despair, but I do know what it feels like to be plateaued. Stuck. Not moving ahead, not sure this is the way things are supposed to be, not uncomfortable enough to change them. Better to deal with the known evil than with the new, unknown one.

So whatever affection they might have had for each other gradually seeped away until the only thing that kept them together was routine, habit: the demands of the family and the house and all the rest of it. The classic American story. She thinks he had affairs, but she doesn't have any evidence. She did tell me that they hardly ever slept together again after that New Year's Eve when he got drunk and shot his mouth off in front of his boss.

Or maybe it's not that simple.

She called me. It was a few days after the New Year began: perhaps that was the coincidence that prompted her. Don't know, didn't ask. I was just so surprised to get the call.

"Phone for you," said Maggie on the intercom. "A Kay McGuire. Should I tell her you're in court this morning?"

"I'll take it," I said, and waited, hanging on every click, while Maggie transferred the call.

The hiss of long distance, and a small voice saying, "Hello?"

"Hello?" I said as loudly as I thought prudent. "Mrs. McGuire?"

"Yes," she said.

"Jason's mother?"

"Yes."

This is the case that won't go away. After we lost in Criminal Appeals, I filed for a rehearing and a stay of execution. The stay was granted, and we still haven't heard anything about the rehearing, although there's no reason to think they'll grant it. It's not like the vote was close, or new information has come to light.

But I do not want Jason to die; it's hard to imagine a more emphatic loss for a lawyer than to have his client get electrocuted. So there is still the U.S. Supreme Court, and if that fails, petitions for postconviction relief in state court, and, if necessary, another pitch to Criminal Appeals; then habeas corpus in federal court, and to the Twelfth Circuit, and to the Supreme Court again. I can keep this thing going a while at least. A long while.

Not that Jason wants me to. I drove up to see him a few

days after Christmas, even though he's an asshole. Caroline had made him some fudge and saved a few sugar cookies from the ravenous and brilliantly manipulative Morton Kondracke.

"Thanks," he said.

"My wife made it," I said.

"Your wife," he said, and looked at me. "I didn't know you were married."

"Of course I'm married," I said. "I have a daughter."

"You look young," he said simply.

You look young.

"We gave her a kitten and a puppy for Christmas," I said. "Want to see a picture?" I fumbled around in my briefcase for the Polaroid snapshots—of Morton Kondracke licking Jessie's face, of Dawn taking a swipe at a glass ornament hanging from the tree, or looking at the camera with deep suspicion. Does Jason even know who Morton Kondracke is, I wondered? The real person?

"I don't want to die," he said. He looked sad and vulnerable and beaten and I couldn't recall the last time I had felt sympathy for him. Never seen him look that way before. The wonderful holiday season does funny things to people.

I was going to tell him his mother had written me, but perhaps it would be cruel to bring the subject up. Christmas on death row, mother and sister God knows where—who wants to be reminded of all that?

"Jason," I said, "look. We still have a lot of cards to play, and one of them's going to come up right. Believe me."

"Please," he said, and for a moment I was sure he was going to start crying.

"Don't worry," I said. "I'm with you all the way. I'll be back to see you next week.'

"You're going?"

"Have to."

*   *   *

"Got your card," I said. "The Christmas card. Where are you?"

"I can't tell you that," she said nervously.

"Why not?"

"I just can't," she said. "Have you seen Jason?"

"Last week."

"How is he?"

"OK," I said.

"I heard about the appeal."

"Tough break," I said. "But the war's a long way from lost. I'm sure things'll come out right in the end."

"You can't let my boy die, Mr. Delafield," she said. "You can't. Please."

"I'm doing everything I can," I said gently.

"I'm sure you are," she said.

A heavy pause.

"Mrs. McGuire," I said, "if there's something you know about this case that might help us, you've got to let me know. Please. Every day counts."

"I can't," she said weakly, and there was a click on the line.

I go down to the steam room and sit there for a while, letting the aggravation run out of me, down my chest and thighs. The purge of frustrations. Calls like that—what can you do? I can't remember feeling more helpless and irrelevant: Can't call her, can't find her, don't know what it is she has to tell me, or if she will; don't know if she'll ever even call again.

It was sweet of Caroline to make the fudge for Jason. She has been a little cold to me for weeks, punishing me for my frivolity in visiting him; but when she asked what was being done for him for Christmas and I said, "Nothing," that got to her.

"He's just sitting there?" she said. "On death row all by himself?"

"So far as I know," I said. "Standard procedure. I don't suppose Santa schedules a stop there."

"Where does his mother live?"

"If I knew that," I said, "I'd be down there already."

She went out that afternoon for the baker's chocolate and the butter and the walnuts and all the rest.

The steam clouds things up nicely and the lights are quite dim, so it's difficult to see very far. I do see the door swing open at the far end of the room, however, and a shadowy form enters.

"Hey, Bryan."

"Brett."

He sits down on the pine bench a few feet away from me, gracefully slipping his towel from around his waist as he does so.

"You're sure here late."

I am. Late for supper; Caroline will be pissed. But there is something womblike about this room, and I have found that when I am in it I simply stop thinking. Today that is an agreeable condition.

"Yes."

He goes on talking in a soft, low voice, murmuring, soothing; I don't quite make out what he's saying—something about a toxic tort case I know his group is struggling with, stuff leaking out of the city's landfill—but I grunt when it seems appropriate and let the words, the steam, the darkness bathe me. I close my eyes.

When I open them a few moments later, I notice that he is lying on his side on the bench, one bent leg jutting into the steamy air. Absently he runs his hands along his thighs, over the shadows of his groin, up his belly.

"God this is great," he says. "I just feel totally relaxed, like I haven't been sitting there all day at a desk."

"Reborn."

"Yeah. Exactly. Sweat it all out. All glisteny. Like those guys in *GQ.*" A little chuckle. He rubs his arms slowly and deeply, moves his neck around. "I get kinks all over," he says. "In my neck and stuff."

"I know what you mean," I say. "Aren't you glad you're a lawyer?"

"We need a masseuse here," he says jokingly. "Or a masseur. Which ever one's a girl."

"Masseuse," I say, glad to be of use.

"I could use a great rubdown."

"Me too," I say.

He brushes a hand across his groin. "Something for the partners to take up at their next meeting," he says. "For now I guess we'll just have to suffer."

I almost offer to give him a massage, but do not. Don't know how. At length he pulls himself upright, shakes his hair, stands, wraps his towel as best he can around his middle, and takes a step toward the door.

"You'll be OK in here?" he says. "You don't want to pass out or something."

"I'll be fine," I say. "But thank you."

"Sure thing. I'm off to the showers. See you tomorrow."

The door swings open, shut. He is gone. Steam puffs in this eternal twilight. I ponder my own muscles; whether he was serious about the firm springing for a masseuse. Masseur. Whichever. Not a bad idea, really.

Jessie is sliding down the bank at the edge of the driveway on her little sled, which is nothing more than a sheet of stiff plastic. She whooshes a good six feet, into the frozen remains of the Whittakers' vegetable garden, Morton Kondracke bounding clumsily after her. Caroline stands by watchfully.

"Hi," I say, getting out of the car.

"Some of us got a little restless," she says.

"So I see. Where's Dawn?"

"Scratching the legs off the kitchen table."

"Well," I say. "We've wanted a new one anyway."

We stand there for a while in the cold while Jessie exhausts herself scrambling up the tiny slope and skidding down it. At last Caroline says, "Enough" and "Daddy's home," and I receive a hug from my daughter and a peck on the lips from my wife and we go inside.

"We ate already," Caroline says. "I'll put yours in the microwave."

It's chicken: rubbery, glutinous, not all that warm or tasty, but I eat it hungrily. I am hungry. Also tired. Caroline gets Jessie ready for bed while I eat. Dawn and Mort remain in my custody—trapped in the kitchen where their mischief can be regulated.

"Will Dawn the cat be declawed and spayed by the end of this month—yes or no, I ask you M. Kondracke?" This in my most jesuitical tone.

Mort looks up at me, tail wagging, pink tongue flopping out. He is either thinking about his answer or hoping that some of my dinner will somehow end up on the floor where he can get it. Clearly he is developing an unhealthy taste for people food. I remind myself to speak to Caroline about this.

Dawn crouches atop the breadbox, as though she knows that Morton and I were discussing her surgery.

"The answer is no," I say. "*No* surgery by the end of this month. Mort, once again you've lurched uncontrollably into the truth."

"I'm exhausted," I say. Also desperately horny. I do not mention this.

"Rough day?"

"Rough day. Talked to Jason's mother."

"You found her?" Real interest in her voice.

"No," I say, "she called me."

"And?"

"Nothing. She hung up on me. She wants to tell me something but she just can't."

"Poor lady," Caroline says. "What a life she's having."

"I didn't know what to do," I say, "so I went to the steam room after work to relax. That's why I was late."

"It's OK."

My hand is tracing the outlines of one of her breasts, circling the nipple, teasing it through the fabric of her nightshirt. My dick is bulging in my jockey shorts. With one hand I start to slip them off and with the other work on the buttons of her shirt. I am about three quarters of the way through the first operation and halfway through the second when she pushes my hand away.

"I'm really tired, too," she says.

"It's only going to take a minute," I say. "Believe me."

"Is that supposed to make me reconsider?"

"You are my wife," I say, though I am not at all sure what I mean by this.

"Bryan In-a-Minute," she says. "Take care of it yourself."

"What's with you tonight?"

"Nothing," she says, turning out her light. "I'm tired. You said you were too. So let's just go to sleep, shall we?" She lays her head on the pillow, back toward me, and I'm lying there with a huge hard-on about three strokes from coming, feeling really steamy. But I'm not going to give her the pleasure. I wait until her breathing becomes deep and steady, and then with a few vicious strokes I jack off onto the sheets. On her side. Dreamless sleep follows.

11

Jason thinks. Not much else to do. Bryan sends him books to read, magazines, writes him letters, but they don't come every day and don't fill up the empty hours, the empty days they do come. He sits there in his cell and thinks.

Patrick, he thinks, I wanted to be like you. I wanted to do everything you did. To be able to throw a curve ball. Do you know that?

A McGuire family vacation, late 1970s. Jimmy Carter is president of the United States. Stagflation. Gasoline costing upwards of $1.25 a gallon. "National malaise." But the family packs into the big Ford station wagon anyway, and sets off west to see the sights. Three weeks cruising the continent, living in motels, eating hamburgers and fried chicken and milkshakes for every meal. A child's paradise. Hell for parents. When little boys have to pee, all else is secondary.

Jason and Patrick divide the back seat between them. There are numerous border altercations: Patrick, being

older, is an imperialist dog; also loud to complain when
Jason attempts to retaliate. Kay is forever leaning over the
front seat to tell them to keep quiet, their father was trying
to drive, did they want to cause an accident? They eat candy
bars and play a game of identifying the different makes of
cars on the road. Jason is good at this, better than Patrick,
and there are some tense moments when Jason wins
decisively.

"Riviera!" he shouts. "Gremlin! Fiesta!"

Patrick is accustomed to dominate in all aspects of life.
He does not take well to being defeated.

In the Black Hills Patrick gets his thumb slammed in
the car door by Jason, who is in a hurry for a soda. Patrick's
face contorts, but he doesn't cry. Don spanks Jason for
being reckless and endangering the safety of his brother.
Patrick, as a reward for his stoicism, gets his picture taken
with Don in front of Mount Rushmore. Father and son;
hand resting on head. Then they play a quick game of catch
while Jason drinks a Coke and is dragged by Kay through
the gift shop.

The country seems to drag on endlessly—an un-
bounded panorama of golden prairie, toothy mountains
washed in lavender and peach at the horizon. The car
smells like new vinyl, which is just the thing when you're
buying it but becomes oppressive after hours and hours in
the dull summer heat of the plains. The boys are forever
wanting to know how much farther; Don is forever saying,
We're almost there. Almost is forever out here. And hot.

Except in the Rockies, where they encounter a mountain thunderstorm so fierce it forces them off the road for
ten minutes. Jason and Patrick roll their windows down to
feel the stinging rain. Kay stares nervously at the weather,
at Don; she has never seen anything like this.

"Don't worry," he says gruffly. "It's just rain. We'll be

rolling in a little while." And so they are. Down and down and down, weaving through the steep valleys of the Wasatch, shadowed and piny, into Salt Lake City. It's an exhilarating ride down the mountain, and fast, but not fast enough for Jason, who shits his pants just before they get off the freeway.

"I smell something," Don says. "Jesus Christ."

"Jason," Kay says, "did you have a little accident?"

"He did it in his pants," Patrick says, chortling. "Just like a baby."

"I did not," Jason says. But they are pulling over as fast as they can, and everyone is rolling down the windows.

These are the sorts of memories that recur to him, that he turns over and over in his unoccupied mind until it is almost like watching a movie. He lies on his little cot and lets the memories roll, in beautiful, perfect, minute detail; the hours roll by with them. The hours that separate him from Phillip's next visit, or that of the guard, who has taken to joining in the festivities.

Summer, several years later. Washington, D.C., so it's extremely hot, and Don complains. A polar bear melting in the sun. They're here for a long weekend, on their way to New York City to see relatives on the McGuire side. They spend Friday afternoon walking up and down the Mall, from the Lincoln Memorial toward the Washington Monument; they make a long stop at the Air and Space Museum to see the space shuttle and the *Enterprise* from "Star Trek." Kay then marches them over to the National Archives, where they stare blankly at the Declaration of Independence and the Constitution, lying in state on their glass catafalques.

They ride the Metro back to their hotel in Woodley Park and have dinner at a little deli on Connecticut. Patrick insists on going swimming, and Jason follows. Don and Kay watch them from lounge chairs poolside. Kay reads the front page of the *Post;* Don scans the baseball scores. Patrick splashes Jason, holds his head under water. Kay shouts at him.

"Ease off," Don tells her. "They're just having fun. That's the way boys are."

When they go back up to the room for bed, Jason is sniffling and his eyes are red. It's the chlorine, he says and locks himself in the bathroom for quite a while. The hotel room is dark and smells of cooled air and fresheners.

When he comes out, Patrick and Don are lying on one of the big queen-sized beds watching CNN sports. Kay is on the other bed, looking at a map of the District, trying to figure out what they can see tomorrow, where they can go, what they can do. Jason climbs onto the bed beside her.

"Tomorrow," he says, "can we go see the pandas?"

"Yes, dear," she says, and he falls asleep snuggled against her. He doesn't wake up later, when she gets up and goes into the bathroom to get ready for bed, and Don gently lifts the sleeping Patrick and sets him down beside his younger brother. He tucks them in as best he can, pats each of them on the head, and plops onto the other bed. By the time Kay emerges from the bathroom, she's the only one still awake.

It has been a bad winter. One by one they are led away, through the green doors in the middle of the night, and new people take their places. Some of them had been there for years, since Jason was a tiny little boy driving down the Wasatch with his family: appealing, appealing, looking for the legal angle that will save them. Each loss adds to the silence of the place. It is like drifting toward a waterfall, knowing it's out there somewhere, not too far away, not knowing how far away or how fast the current is carrying you. Just like the real world, except that the falls are a lot closer, the roar growing in your ears, and you know you'll be all there when the moment comes.

Seven gone since Halloween. One November night two were taken away.

"Dear Mom," he writes,

> I hope you and Colleen had a nice Christmas. I thought about you a lot. We had roast beef here, and ice cream, so that was nice. No tree, though.
>
> Sometimes I wish you would come visit but I can understand why you don't. Sometimes I wish you would write, too, but I can understand that you really don't have anything to say to me. I just want to know that you and Colleen are all right.
>
> Happy New Year.
>
> > Love,
> > Jason

It wasn't a Christmas to write home about, all the same. Dinner arrived unheralded on the tray, as usual. Gray roast beef slathered in gravy. Mashed potatoes. Soggy broccoli. Vanilla ice cream dyed green and red represented the prison administration's sole concession to the holiday season. Jason sat on his little cot and ate it; afterward one of the guards took him outside briefly to see the snow fall.

Is Santa coming? No, but there is a commotion in the middle of the night, shoes scraping on the concrete floor, a key rattling in the lock, the cell door squealing on its neglected hinges. Jason awakes, knows instantly. He tenses but does not move: there is no place to move to. No place to hide. He waits for the darting hands, the hot mouth, the cock working like a piston—but nothing. He waits.

There is a flaring sound and a brief orange flash in the darkness. Then the sound of someone puffing on a cigarette. Phillip doesn't smoke. Phillip doesn't wait. As discreetly as possible, Jason opens his eyes a crack and tries to figure out who it is.

It's hard to see in the darkness, hard to make out anything but a silhouette framed by stale yellow light. The cigarette glows; the breath is slow and deep and easy. Calm. Jason's beating heart slows from gallop to brisk trot.

Go away, he thinks, oh God go away.

It's midnight. Is Gretchen waiting? Did I forget something? Did they not tell me when it was going to happen? Surprise, Jason! We thought it would be easier for you this way.

He squeezes his eyes shut again, counts slowly to fifty. Very slowly. Go away, he thinks. Forty-nine. Go away. Fifty. A deep breath. The silhouette is still there, motionless. The cell smells like cigarette smoke now. Panic rising. Just fuck me, whoever you are, fuck me and let's get it over with. "Fuck me": the words form on his lips. He almost says them, wants to shout them.

A foot shuffles, then another. Whoever it is is approaching. Jason braces. He can feel the figure leaning over him, regarding him, plotting its strategy. He steals a peek through cracked eyelids, and he recognizes the man. It's the guard who let Phillip in the first time. He's not very old, not too savvy. He is the Jason of guards.

The guard squats, so that his face is no more than a foot from Jason's. The smell of his breath is sharp, smoky: it smells like Patrick's when he'd been fooling around, as he sometimes did, with cigarettes. Puffing them in the woods, then munching Ritz crackers to conceal the smell.

Mutterings. Jason can't make them out. The guard could be talking to him or to himself. Is he humming?

Christmas carols? Not the plummiest assignment: grave-yard shift, death row, Christmas Eve, the rest of the family home vaguely worried, eager for the morning and your safe homecoming. Jason almost feels bad for him. The turkey will be in the oven by the time you get home, or the ham, and the smell of it will fill the kitchen and the whole house. You will even be able to smell it outside as you get out of your car and trudge up the walk to the door.

"You awake, man?"

Keep your breathing deep and steady. Think about sleep, think about being relaxed. Keep your breath nice and steady.

"You awake?"

Gently he touches Jason's face, runs the back of his fingers along Jason's cheek. He brushes his eyelids, runs his hands along the outlines of Jason's ear. Jason waits, mind blank.

This is familiar territory, after all. After the first time with Phillip, the guard became less cautious and in subsequent meetings joined in the fun. They took turns.

The guard runs his hands through Jason's short, stubbly hair, cradles his head in his hands. His breathing is slow and sad.

"I'm glad you're asleep, man," he says in a throaty whisper, "cause you won't have to listen to me talk. I'll talk to you a little just the same. I'm sorry about what's happenin' to you here. I mean about Phillip and everything. It's hard to explain. I just got carried away, I'm sorry. It's just that watching him do it to you—I don't know. I'll try to keep him off you."

I've got a brother who's no older than you, he thinks, who barely shaves, whose skin is still soft like a baby's. He's home now, asleep, waiting for Christmas morning to come, and although he's too old to believe in Santa Claus, he looks forward to the bright morning sun, the light glinting off the snow and the glass ornaments hanging from the tree, the smell of turkey wafting from the oven. He looks forward to reading the paper while our dad builds a fire in the fireplace, mom bringing out the kringle and the orange juice and coffee for a simple family breakfast—a respite before the guests start to show up.

I'll be looking forward to all that stuff, too, when I bust out of here in a few hours and head home. When I get to go back to the world.

He leans over slowly and brushes Jason's lips with his own; he rubs his fingers softly over the boy's brow.

"Merry Christmas," he whispers. "Sleep tight."

It is only after Jason is sure that he's gone and has locked the cell door behind him, that no one is out there watching, only then does he allow himself to double up in silent sobs of relief. Regret.

12

Bryan meets her in a little wine bar at O'Hare Airport. The bar is a tiny oasis in the desert of concourses, gates, ticket counters, escalators, electric carts, travelers, pickpockets that is O'Hare; a little tuft of potted palm trees and glass tables and $4-a-glass California zinfandels and chardonnays.

She is already sitting there, at a little table in the corner, sipping a spritzer, when Bryan strides in. He's been driving for hours over roads spotted with ice; the traffic around the airport is hell; he's ready to sit down and relax a moment. But he knows he can't, knows that she will be waiting for him. That was the deal they made, so he wouldn't know when she arrived, or from where.

She called again, a week or two after their first phone conversation. He was brusque at first, unable to pick up on her game, but her meek determination dissolved into sniffles and he stood there holding the phone, feeling like a cad.

"Why do you keep calling me?"

"I don't know."

"I think you do," he said. "Why don't you tell me?"

"I can't," she said. "Not over the phone."

"Then let's meet. I'll fly out to see you. Wherever you are."

"No," she said in the strongest voice he'd ever heard her use. "No. Let's meet somewhere. Can you do that?"

"Sure. Say where and when."

He recognizes her immediately: she looks like a woman who's been through the sort of hard times one would hesitate to ask about. Her complexion is pale, despite some sunburn, and slightly pocked; her reddish hair is washed-out and streaked with gray in a way that is not flattering or distinguished. Like March snow: tired. Her eyes were blue once, bleary now, blue still but devoid of color.

There is no question that it is her.

"Mrs. McGuire?" he says gently, extending a hand. "Bryan Delafield. I'm Jason's lawyer."

She rises wearily to shake Bryan's hand. Her skin is cool and clammy, her grip limp.

"I'm glad you could come," she says simply.

"I'm glad you could come."

The waiter comes to take Bryan's order. He asks for a glass of zinfandel and a small basket of pretzels.

"How's my boy?" she asks.

"He's all right," Bryan says. He wants to go on, but all the clichés of vernacular discourse—"He really likes it there," "He's making a lot of friends," "It's a good place for him right now," the sorts of things parents say about their college-age children—seem inappropriate. "I see him when I can. I know," he continues gently, "that he'd like to see you."

"I can't see him," she says with a sigh that blows out of

her crumpled heart. "Just can't. Colleen and I have got to get on with things. Jason—he could eat us up. I know that must sound awful to you," she says, her eyes turning directly on him, flashing just a bit for the first time, "like I'm cruel or don't love him. I do love him, Mr. Delafield, with all my heart. But he's lost and there's nothing I can do to save him."

"I hope he's not lost," Bryan says softly. "I'm doing everything I can to prevent it."

"I don't mean just . . . that," she says. "I mean, the whole thing. Even if they don't kill him, he'll spend his whole life in prison. There's nothing left of the family. It might not have been much of a family, but at least it was something. Now it's just Colleen and me."

The wine and pretzels come. Bryan takes a long sip of the burgundy liquid, slips a pretzel stick into his mouth.

"He writes you letters, you know," he says. "Every week. Wonders why you don't answer."

"I don't get them," she says. "He doesn't have the new address and the mail doesn't get forwarded from the old one. Sometimes I want to send him something," she continues in an unfocused tone, "a box of cookies or something. A card for his birthday. But I don't. There's nothing to say."

A pause.

"Not to him, maybe," Bryan says. "What about to me?"

"Well," she says slowly, and he can see tears welling. She pulls a tissue from her purse and dabs at her nose. "It just about broke my heart, Mr. Delafield."

"What did?"

"Everything. That morning. Finding them. Jason in the kitchen. I was afraid something like this was going to happen. It was bound to. And the trial—all of them wanting my baby boy's blood, when they had no clue what was happening. They didn't care. Oh my, that's hard to live with. I couldn't stay in Batavia any more, not after reading that paper and hearing what people said about my son, what they thought about my husband. They're good people but they just couldn't understand."

"What couldn't they understand?"

"Mr. Delafield," she says. "You've got to save him. He doesn't deserve to die. Lots of criminals do, I believe—you probably don't agree with me, living in Monroe and everything—but Jason doesn't. He was trying to save himself."

"Mrs. McGuire," Bryan says, "Kay. I don't understand what you mean."

"It's hard to talk about."

"Try."

"All right," she says at length. "For him. But it's not easy to talk about. It's not easy to live with."

"I know."

"I don't actually *know* anything," she says. "For a fact, I mean. I mean, I never saw anything, nobody ever told me anything. But I know in my heart, Mr. Delafield, if you can believe that."

"I can," Bryan says patiently. He is used to these sorts of tortured, circuitous revelations, knows how to coax the secrets out of hiding. Don't demand, don't insist, don't get impatient. Just let it emerge at its own pace. "Would you like another drink?" he asks.

"I don't think so,' she says, Then: "Maybe one more."

Bryan motions to the waiter.

"You felt something to be true even though you never saw it, is that right, Kay?" he says after placing the order.

"It is," she says.

"Sometimes," he says, "we feel more than we know" and feels, in saying so, that he has been wiser than he intended to be. It's true, he thinks: feelings, intuitions, don't lie.

"Oh, Mr. Delafield," she says, "you're so right about that. I always felt that I knew my husband, knew what he wanted, even though we weren't getting along that well."

"When he died?"

"For a long time before."

"Fighting?"

"No," she says, "not exactly. Not shouting or anything like that. I think we didn't especially care for one another anymore but still knew each other well from all those years together. You're married?"

"Yes."

"You know what I mean."

"Maybe a little."

"You just know when something's not right. Of course, for us things hadn't been right for years—for most of the marriage, in fact. We didn't even sleep in the same room anymore, let alone the same bed."

"What about Colleen?"

"Oh, occasionally he would come in, if he was in the mood, and sometimes I let him stay. If I was in the mood. Sometimes he would pound on the door and yell at me to let him in, but I wouldn't. That was at first. Later he got used to it."

"Why the separate bedrooms?"

"Oh, Mr. Delafield," she says, "I was just tired of him."

"Did he have affairs?"

"Before or after?"

"I don't know," Bryan says. "Either."

"No," she says slowly, "not that I know of. I might have been able to understand if that's what he'd been up to."

"What is it you can't understand?"

She pauses, and he thinks she is thinking what to say, but then he notices that her eyes are dripping tears and her breath is coming hard to her.

"Patrick," she manages to say in a choked voice.

"Patrick."

Jason spoke in a whisper toward the other bed. He couldn't tell if Patrick were in it or not. The blankets were all crumpled and the pillows piled here and there.

"Are you there?"

No answer. Jason stared at the ceiling and thought about how to get out of Batavia, wondered what lay beyond the town, in the rest of Columbia, the world. He had heard good things about Monroe; maybe he would go there after he got out of school.

I don't want to live here, he thought, not in this little town with my parents. The McGuires, senior, were a cautionary tale in Jason's fifteen-year-old eyes—young eyes, but no longer those of a child. They were unhappy and frustrated, with each other and everything else. Even he could see that. The separate bedroom thing hadn't bothered him much a few years ago, when it started, but now it struck him as bizarre. Ominous.

A bolt of light hit him in the face, then darkness again. Movements across the room.

"Is that you?"

"Yeah."

"Where've you been?"

"Talking to Dad."

Jason saw him now, a shadowy figure in white jockey shorts, moving around on his bed, arranging the pillows, smoothing out the sheets.

"In Dad's room?"

"Yeah." A flash of annoyance. "Where do you think?"

"I don't know. What were you talking about?"

"Nothing special," said Patrick. "Just stuff."

Yes. That was their way, their bond. Don and Jason seldom talked about anything. Patrick and Jason talked about what Don and Patrick had been doing. There was a weird symmetry to the whole thing.

"Oh."

There was a long interval in which Jason began to drift off to sleep. It was hard for him to sleep when Patrick wasn't there; he was used to his brother's presence, his smell, and when he was gone Jason couldn't fall asleep because he couldn't stop wondering when Patrick would come in.

"You ever fucked a girl?"

Patrick's voice broke through the still darkness, and Jason started at the sound of it.

"What?"

"I said, have you ever fucked a girl?"

"What time is it?"

"Who cares what time it is?" Patrick said. "It's twelve thirty. Have you?"

"No," Jason admitted. "Have you?"

"Almost," Patrick said. "Girls like to tease."

"Yeah. They do."

"They get you real horny and then kiss you good night."

"Yeah," said Jason, who had yet to kiss a girl.

"You know what I mean?"

"Yeah."

"Are you horny now?"

"Not really," Jason said. He had jacked off earlier, waiting for Patrick to come back from wherever it was he had gone.

"I am."

"Oh."

A rustling in the darkness. Suddenly Patrick was right on top of him.

"I have a feeling it started with Don and Patrick," she says.

"How do you know?"

"I can just feel it," she says. "Don was lonely. I guess that was my fault. I drove him to it. Where was he going to turn?"

"To his elder son?" Bryan is incredulous. She can't have gotten this right, he thinks. These sorts of things don't really happen. Father and son? Brothers? He suppresses a shiver. "What about Jason?"

It was a sharp pain that seemed to shoot all through him. Patrick's body over his, sweaty, suffocating: he wanted to scream but Patrick said that he and Dad would kill him if he made trouble.

"Dad will not," Jason said. "Dad would really be pissed if he knew what you were doing."

"Would he?" Patrick said. "Relax. Don't fight it."

Jason could have fought him off; they were about the same size, and Jason had fought him off before. All he had to do was grab his balls and squeeze, or pull his hair, and that would be the end of it. But he did not do any of those things. He couldn't stop thinking about what Patrick had said.

Patrick came in half a dozen animal grunts and slid off him, exhausted and sleepy.

"I don't believe what you said about you and Dad killing me," he said. "And I'm never going to let you do that to me again."

"Tell him all about it," Patrick said.

Later that night the door creaked open again.

"You're saying," Bryan says, "what?"

"I never saw anything," says Kay, sniffling. "But I heard. I could tell."

"Heard what?"

"The same things Colleen heard," she says. "The noises she talked about at the trial. She thought he was beating them up. I knew what he was really doing to them."

A look of horror crosses her face, and he understands that she cannot describe what she means, cannot form the awful words.

He nods. "You really believe that?"

"Yes," she says in a voice so soft that he is reading her lips rather than listening to her.

"Why?"

"Did he ever tell you any of this?"

"Jason? No."

"How do you know for sure that this was going on?"

"Mr. Delafield, I know."

"You never saw anything."

"No."

"No one told you anything."

"No. But I know it's true, all the same."

Bryan considers the wine in front of him. The goblet is almost empty, and he feels the heat of the alcohol spreading through his limbs. Another glass and he will be enveloped in that warm haze in which one's troubles seem to blur and vanish. Also unfit to drive. He motions to the waiter for more pretzel sticks.

"Forgive me for asking, Mrs. McGuire," he says, "but if you knew this was going on, for God's sake why didn't you do anything about it?"

She stares at him, and he can't tell if she's about to cry or slap his face. She does neither. At length she says, "He was a big, strong man, Mr. Delafield. What was I going to do? Call the police on him?"

"He was committing a terrible crime," Bryan says, "and he deserved to be punished."

"I know," she says miserably, and now she is crying a little—not for the first time, though he cannot know that.

13

I am in a tizzy as I pay the bill and leave Kay McGuire to her thoughts and the flight back to wherever it is she came from. An absolute tizzy. It occurs to me that she may be making the whole thing up, may have taken Colleen's fanciful reports too much to heart and given them a particularly horrible gloss.

Also a gloss from which I cannot seem to distract my attention. If the story is true, I can't believe it. How could two strong young men allow themselves to be used by their father in such an unspeakable way? How could a father—any father—do that to his children? The most astonishing images cross my mind.

No wonder he did it. Who wouldn't flip out after a while, playing the bottom rung on a sexual totem pole? Your mother won't help you, there's nobody else in the family to turn to. He should have gone to the police. Somebody should have.

Unless the whole story is made up. Unless she's trying to protect him, for whatever sick reason, trying to plant in my mind an explanation for an interval of brutality that even jaded cops found sickening. She has stumbled late on a means of reviving her son's reputation, but she has stumbled on it nonetheless, and what better way to try it out than to feed it to the lawyer. He's hungry for some sympathetic news, he'd like to believe that his client isn't a total beast. Clue him in.

I am so confused as I leave the airport that I nearly drive through the toll plaza without paying.

It is a long drive back to Monroe, and I do not get there until after nightfall. The sky is clear and black tonight, and the sight of the capitol building, its white marble dome brilliantly illuminated, shining across the flat expanse of the frozen lake, stirs me. I am glad to be back here. Already the day seems like a bad dream.

Caroline and Jessie have gone out, says the note; back before nine. Morton Kondracke is penned up in the kitchen and in his loneliness has made two messes on the linoleum. The housebreaking program appears to have reached a plateau. At first I am inclined to bawl him out, but he is so clearly glad to see me, see anyone—the little tail wagging frantically, the tongue out, the little yips of joy—that I can't. Instead I say, "Come on, Mort," and let him out the garage door into the front yard. He romps around a while but never goes more than a few steps without looking for me and yelping. He is glad of my company, not afraid to show it; and I am glad of his.

The most chilling thing about my day with Mrs. McGuire is that it makes me worry about Jessie. That is selfish, yes, but honest of me to admit to myself that that was the first thing I thought of when she told me about the men in that godawful house. What must it feel like to be a parent, to know something like that is going on, and not be able to stop it? Not, for that matter, even try?

How could she not try? Why wasn't she the one the police found sitting in the kitchen, holding the bloody knife? If I thought anyone was doing something like that to Jessie, I wonder if anything could control me. Just the thought of it, the mere abstraction, makes the hate well up in me.

I hate her. She's weak, ineffective, in a fundamental way unprincipled. She was willing to let that beast do whatever he wanted, wreck the family, rape the boys and their lives—she wouldn't stop him because she was afraid he would slap her around. He never slapped anybody around. He wasn't that kind of guy. He was basically gentle and sick. But his size intimidated, and I guess the enormity of what he was doing intimidated, too.

The question is whether or not to believe her. It's such a horrible story that part of me says it can't be true. On the other hand, her telling casts her in such an unfavorable light that it's hard to believe she could make it up. A "declaration against interest," as lawyers are fond of saying.

There's only one way to find out. And even that might not work. And if it does, then what?

"Come on, Mort," I say, and he bounds up to chew on my shoelace. I pick him up and carry him in; as I do so he nuzzles my face.

"I understand," Caroline says calmly. We are lying in bed; the "Tonight Show" is on but the sound is turned off.

"You do?" It's hard to suppress my surprise. My trips to Warrensville have not generally met with her favor. And in the middle of a Columbia winter there's always the matter of threatening weather. But there is no doubt in her voice, no irony.

"Yes," she says. "My God. What if it's true? I mean, what if that were Jessie? I would want her lawyer to find out everything he could."

"Well," I say, "no telling what I'm going to find out."

"What if it's true?" she says. "What will you do then?"

"I don't think it's true," I say. "I think she's gone half out of her mind."

"It is a bizarre story," she agrees.

"Too bizarre."

We lie there for a while, half embracing, thinking. Thinking about rapes and prisons and parents and children and bloody murder. Thinking about fathers and sons and wondering why. Do I feel this way for the same reason people scream with delight when a hockey game degenerates into a bloody fight? Voyeurism? Can't shake the images.

"You know, Bryan," she says at length, "I love you. I'm glad we're safe here, the three of us."

"Me too," I say, and I am wondering how safe we really are when sleep comes.

Jason does not seem thrilled to see me. Once his attitude made me nervous; that first day I met him his unfriendliness upset me so much that I had to take two Maalox and sit in the car for fifteen minutes before I felt well enough to drive. He can be amazingly unpleasant.

Today he is not being unpleasant at that level—just indifferent, mildly churlish. As though he senses the purpose of my visit.

"Hi," I say.

"Hi." Looks at his fingers, drums them on the table.

"How've you been?"

"Fine."

Me, too, I think, and thanks for asking. Always nice to know that people care about you. But why should I care if this little snot cares about me? Who needs that kind of goodwill?

"That's good," I say. "I suppose we should get right down to business. I saw your mother two days ago."

The drumming stops. He looks at me, cocks his head slightly. No comment.

"I met her in Chicago. At the airport, actually."

"Where's she living?"

"I don't know," I say. "We didn't get into that."

"You didn't get her address, man?" he says. "Boy, you are some lawyer. Has she gotten my letters?"

"I don't know," I say, hedging as best I can. "I don't think so. Maybe some of them. But that wasn't why I met her."

"Did you tell her to write to me?"

"Jason," I say, "please. I'll do everything I can to put you in touch with her. But first there's an important matter we have to discuss. It came up in my conversation with her and I need to talk it over with you."

"Fuck," he says, and shifts around in his chair. "Nothing important you could have talked about with her."

"She told me about your father," I say evenly.

"What about him?"

"And your brother."

"What about him?"

"And you."

"What about me?"

"About what was going on between the three of you."

"I don't know what you're talking about," he says.

"It's not true, then?" I look at this young man across the

table from me, try to imagine him pinned naked to a bed, a body just like his, only a year or two older, on top of him. It is a fantastic image, ludicrous, and I almost burst out laughing at the thought that I have believed it. I have believed Jason's mother's tale, her invention to absolve her son morally if not legally. It was brilliant—a soap bubble dazzling in the sunshine—but it has just popped into nothing.

"Don't have any idea what you're talking about, man," he says more or less into his left shoulder.

What a waste of time this is. The whole thing. The truth is that Jason McGuire is just a nutty little thug who got a big kick out of killing half his family. Someday we may figure out what drives people to commit crazy murders like this. Maybe it's in the genes or the baby food they get. In the meantime, for our purposes, they are responsible for what they do: they are lucid, they are intelligent. They did it, they meant to do it, and they should go to the chair forthwith. Let's be rid of them. Let's be rid of him, at least.

"Just for the record," I say, "she told me that your father and your brother sexually assaulted you over a period of many months. That they raped you, in other words. That's not true, you say."

"It's a goddamn fucking lie," he says in a voice quiet but so intense that I half expect the guard to come back into the room and lead him off in chains. "It's a *fucking* lie. You can't believe a fucking word that bitch says, man. Just tell her to go to fucking hell. Why the fuck would she tell you something like that?"

"I don't know," I say.

He laughs a little, like a crazy man. Herbert Lom in the "Pink Panther" movies. Most unsettling.

"She's a lying whore," he says, almost genially now.

"They never touched you."

"What do you think we were, man, a bunch of faggots? You think we sat around at night playing with each other's meat? Cornholing each other? I'll bet that really turns you on, doesn't it, you little fruit."

"Go to hell," I say, and get up to leave.

"Where are you going?" he says.

"I've got work to do," I say. "I've got a bank appealing a three-and-a-half-million-dollar judgment. What the hell am I doing here?"

"You can't go," he says. "You haven't told me where she's living. Where I can get in touch with her and Colleen."

"I can go any time I damn well please," I say. "And I'm going now. I don't know where she is. You find out."

I stuff my notepad into my briefcase and motion for the guard to open the door. Jason stands up—is he taller than the last time I saw him?—and I know he's going to jump me. He's going to make me tell him something I don't know. He is crazy.

"Please," he says, a bit wildly. "Please don't go. Please don't. I need you to stay here and talk to me a little."

"I've talked to you enough," I say. "You're a lying, murderous little slime ball and I've got better things to do than sit around here listening to you carry on. I've filed the brief for review in the Supreme Court, by the way, so you don't have anyting to worry about for a while."

The taste of these words on my tongue is bitter, agreeably so. *For a while:* say it again? Make the little bastard squirm? I turn to go.

"Bryan," he says. "I need you."

Pause. Arrested by a note in his voice so beguiling and poignant that it is as though he has reached inside me. I remember where I am, what he is facing, what he has done. He is a kid. Doubt.

"Please," he says again. "Just talk to me for a few more minutes. Tell me about something. Tell me about your family. Your wife. Your kid. Just talk to me. Let me hear your voice. Let me hear about you."

"All right," I say, and motion to the guard that I will be a while longer. I sit back down at the table and look at him. He looks at me with those feline eyes, aglow with something. "I don't know what to say to you," I say.

"Do you know you're the only person who comes to visit me?" he says. "I've got cousins and uncles and stuff around here. They don't even answer my letters. You're the only one who even writes to me."

"I do what I can for you," I say. "You're my client. You're in difficult circumstances. It's my job to do everything I can for you."

"I know I don't always show it," he says, "but I know that and I appreciate it. I look forward to your letters and when you come. I think about your face when I'm alone." He shoots me a little grin—not the killer grin, but a boyish one, almost shy—and it occurs to me how much he looks like Brett, the young associate at the office. Odd that I've never seen the resemblance before. "Do you think about me?"

Stiffly: "Yes."

"What does your wife know about me?"

"What does it matter?" I say.

"Just curious."

"To answer your question," I say, "yes, she knows all about you."

"What does she look like, your wife?"

"She's beautiful," I say, almost substituting "dutiful" by accident. It's hard to describe Caroline, why she is attractive. Hard to picture her while I am sitting here in this prison talking to this boy. The image of her is totally incongruous. I show him the photos of Caroline and Jessie I always carry with me in my wallet. "That's them," I say. "My wife and my daughter."

"She's just a little girl," Jason says. "What? Four?"

"Yeah."

"What's the puppy's name?"

"Morton," I say. "He's named after, ah, a friend of my wife's."

"That's nice."

"Jason," I say, "I really have to be going. I'll be in touch."

"Oh," he says in a tiny voice. "You can't talk just a little longer?"

"I don't know what the point is," I say. "I found out what I came here to find out."

I wince a little inside as I say this; it sounds more cruel than I intended. I make it sound as though that's the only reason I came today.

"About my father, you mean."

"Yes."

"Well," he says, and lowers his forehead so that it's resting on his hands, on the tabletop. "I guess you found out."

"Yes."

"Would you stay?" he says, raising his head, "if I told you it was all true?"

"I have to go," I say, and get up and extend my hand toward him. "Goodbye." He does not take my hand.

"Would you?"

"It's not true," I say. "You told me so."

"It is," he says. "I lied."

"You lie a lot. How am I supposed to know when you're telling the truth?"

"You're not," he says. Another smile, this one less benign.

"Five minutes ago you were swearing up a storm at your mother for lying about your dad and your brother. Now you say you're lying. Do you know something?" I say, suddenly furious at him, the manipulative little prick. I point a finger: "I really don't give a shit whether you're lying or not. Whether they fucked you or not. I'm sick of you and this whole damn scene and I'm gone."

I motion to the guard and storm out of the room as grandly as I can. I am so pleased with my performance of outrage that I don't hear him call out one last time for me to stay. I am so pleased that it doesn't occur to me that I still have no idea what, if anything, might have happened between Jason and Patrick and Don.

I will think about that tonight, on the long drive back to Monroe.

14

Saturday night the Delafields treat themselves to a night out. A babysitter is procured for little Jessie and Morton and Dawn. Bryan and Caroline take off for dinner, a play, whatever. They need to get out; they know it. Bryan is preoccupied, Caroline senses drift.

"He wouldn't tell me," he told her when he got home that night. "I mean, we went back and forth and back and forth and it was like he was flirting with me, jiggling one answer then another. I have no idea what the truth is. I don't care."

"Of course you care," she said, a little unwillingly, hoping somewhere down deep that he really didn't care. "What's going on with the appeals?" Get back to the legal strategies. Get him away from the boy. Depersonalize the thing, that's the trick. She's never before, as she does now, seen one of his clients exert such a strong emotional pull on him. Who gives a shit about a bank suing another bank, after all, or two insurance companies slugging it out with *in limine* motions?

"I filed the petition for cert last week," he said. "We'll see." He does not mention to her, to anyone, the high likelihood that the Supreme Court will refuse even to hear the matter. The justices have gotten sick of death-penalty appeals. It is a swamp, trackless and soggy: no escape.

"We'll go out tomorrow," she said. "Have some fun."

"OK."

The restaurant is on the city's west side. Its entrance is a set of oak doors surrounded by clear glass bricks. A red and blue neon sign spelling out the restaurant's name—"Parri's"—shines through the bricks left of the door. The maître d' seats them immediately, and they order a bottle of Chandon and a plate of antipasto.

"God," Bryan says. The champagne soothes him, the little bubbles, the elegance of the flute, and he gives a deep sigh of comfort.

"I love this place," Caroline says. "We should come here more often." Read: we should go out more often. They do not lack for money, or even for time; they simply don't go out all that much.

The food comes in waves: little plates of steamed vegetables with garlic dip; a basket of breads and butter; a salad with a spicy pepper cream dressing; some snapper in lime-pepper butter for Caroline and a plate of jambalaya pasta for Bryan. More champagne. They share it all, moving things from plate to plate and making something of a mess on the white tablecloth.

The bill comes and Bryan pays it without quite knowing how much it is. "Just put it on this," he says, handing the waiter his American Express card. The chit comes and he signs. Caroline figures the tip and writes in the total.

*   *   *

Dear Bryan,

I know you think I'm an asshole. Maybe I am. I don't always mean to be—like yesterday when you came to visit. I pissed you off and I didn't even mean to. I know you won't believe that but it's true. I'm sorry and I hope you come again soon so we can talk some more. About whatever you want. I mean that. Is it alright if I call you Bryan? You don't seem like an old lawyer to me.

I'm glad you talked to my mother. I don't really hate her, except sometimes I do. It's hard to explain. I don't know if I can. She's not a bad person. I do love Colleen, though.

I read that book you gave me about the kid who thought he was Superman. It made a lot of sense. Lots of times I've felt the same way. I liked the cat on the back, too.

I really don't have anything more to say.

Jason

Jason sets the pen down on the pencil and reads back what he has written. It is not turning out the way he wants it to. Frustrating to stare at the paper, unable to fill it with the words that express what he wants to express. He is not sure what he wants to express. That makes it all the harder. I wish you were here so I could talk to you face-to-face, he thinks, but he recalls that that's not a perfect solution, either.

Slow footsteps up and down the row. It's ten o'clock; the guards shine their flashlights into each cell, making sure everyone is bedded down for the night. It's been quiet for the past few weeks: no new arrivals on the row, no midnight rendezvous with Gretchen. There is a sense—Jason feels it, mistrusts it, can't resist it—that things have settled down, that they will remain this way indefinitely. It is relief. He has bottomed out. He can rally. The optimism bubbles up intermittently: the Court will grant his petition, will reverse the sentence. Perhaps in not too long he will be eligible for parole.

He will get out of here.

He will find his mother and Colleen. He will visit Bryan at his house, meet his wife, the kid with the dog, eat supper with him. He will find a job somewhere, anywhere but Columbia, where people don't know what he did, or why. Where they won't assume he's evil and shun him. I'm not evil, he thinks.

Possibly a big city. Possibilities in big cities. A need to grow and stretch. The cell is psychologically as well as physically limiting: impossible to feel anything here, to become anything here, to do anything here. Life reduced to a minimum.

All this because no one's been taken away for a midnight meeting.

"I didn't love the play," says Caroline.

"I don't know," says Bryan.

"I liked it," says Brett, who's sitting next to Caroline and across from Bryan. They are all drinking champagne. "It made me laugh."

"You lawyers," Caroline says, "laugh at anything."

"Quite a wife you've got here, boss," Brett says. "Gorgeous and *very* diplomatic."

"I think I'll keep her," Bryan says. The last gossamer strands of sobriety are slipping from his grasp. The world spins slowly; he feels warm, weightless. Brett looks amazingly like Jason. Same nose, darker hair. The voice is different. Eyes not quite the same color; Brett's tending toward blue.

They ran into Brett after the show. He had been there with another associate, Peter Skillus. They share a secretary. Peter went home right after, but Bryan said, We're going to White Knight's for a drink, why don't you join us? and Brett said, What the hell.

"What the hell," says Bryan.

"Great champagne," Brett says to Caroline. "Makes me feel like dancing."

No dancing at White Knights. It is a comfortable bar and restaurant, done up in dark oak, brass, potted plants: a favored gathering place of the downtown crowd. Only steps from the Civic Center, only blocks from the state capitol.

No dancing, but tables full of people talking: undergraduates from the university, there to take advantage of fifty-cent tap beers; families; couples on their way to or from the theater.

"I don't think I want to dance tonight," Bryan says.

"He's depressed about his murderer," Caroline says.

"Yeah?"

"Yeah."

"What about him?"

"He's a lying little scum bag," Bryan says with unexpected lucidity. "His whole family is. We're better off without any of them."

"Bummer," says Brett.

"So, Brett," Caroline says, "how's your love life?"

Brett laughs, looks at Bryan, who's staring off vacantly. "Lawyers don't have love lives," he says. "Isn't that right, Bryan?"

"No," Bryan says, still staring off into space, "I guess not."

"No time," Brett says. "I'm at the office sixty hours a week. You two are lucky you found each other early."

"There must be some eligible young women at the office," Caroline says.

Brett laughs again. "I dunno," he says. "I'm always in the library or writing a brief or on my way to court or something. Isn't that right, boss man?"

"Yes," says Bryan, who's returned to the conversation. "You do work hard. Maybe too hard."

"That's what I think," Caroline says.

"Gotta make partner," Brett says with a smile. Bryan finds himself staring. Odd what you notice when you're drunk. Some things are so much clearer, seem to make sense as they do not when you're sober. Your head feels detached from your body, but you are, in some curious way, still aware of your body. The pressure below your stomach.

"We should go soon," Caroline says. "It's getting late."

"Yes," Brett says.

"Pee," Bryan says. "Back in a minute."

"Me, too," Brett says to Caroline.

The two men move off a bit unsteadily. Caroline reaches for a mint from the bowl on the table.

The light shines on Jason's face. His eyes are open and, like a deer, he doesn't move.

"You awake?" It's the young guard, speaking in a strained whisper. "He's asleep," he whispers to someone else. "Let's go."

"He ain't asleep," says another, rougher voice. "Eyes are wide open. Unlock it."

Phillip.

"Aw, come on, man, he's just a kid. Give him a break."

"Open it."

The cell door swings open. The two figures pass in silently. Jason lies there without resisting; he even helps Phillip pull his underwear off. Phillip fucks him quickly, savagely. It hurts a little but it's all over in about a minute.

Then the heavy body is off him and he hears the two move off. The cell is locked again. Silence. Drift off.

He is jolted awake some time later by the sound of the key in the lock. He lies there without moving while the guard slithers inside, sidles up to the bed. He kneels down and says, "Are you awake, man?"

Jason nods yes.

"You all right?"

Another nod.

"I'm sorry about him," says the guard. "I really am." His voice breaks. "It's just that I can't—I can't—"

Jason shakes his head. Don't worry about it.

"You shouldn't even be here," says the guard, gently stroking Jason's cheek. The boy is still naked, erect now. Stroking himself. The guard feels a flush. So easy to possess this delicate beauty. There for the taking. Jason reaches out and touches him on the lips.

"It's OK."

The guard's pants are down and he's on top of Jason, in Jason, pumping slowly and as sensuously as he knows how. Work it around, side to side, as far in as it'll go, all the way back without the head popping out. The way his girlfriend likes it. It's tighter than fucking a cunt, he thinks, and a lot naughtier. An exciting thought. Beautiful skin, shapely muscles, shiny young hair. For a moment he fantasizes that it is her. Nobody'll ever find out. The kid'll be gone soon enough.

Bryan, Jason thinks, doing himself as the guard fucks, him. Bryan.

So they are standing there at the urinals, side by side, nothing happening.

"Boy," Bryan says, "blitzed."

"Can't go," Brett says. He kneads himself with his right hand, as though that will make the piss issue forthwith. "I gotta go so bad, it's driving me nuts."

"I know what you mean," Bryan says.

They each sneak glances at each other, not too discreetly. Jutting out like lances.

"Wow," Bryan says. Perhaps he is dreaming this. Perhaps he is dreaming what it feels like to have Brett reaching over, stroking him, lightly touching his balls. Room spinning. Head spinning. His own hand straying to Brett, feeling the hot, hard column, squeezing it, feeling a little bit of sticky fluid from the tip smear on his palm. What would it feel like? Hot. Maybe he will wake up now, any second, and find Caroline next to him and the sheets damp and sticky around his waist.

Caroline.

The bathroom door swings open and a pretty blond waiter comes in. They stand there stiffly, at attention. The waiter stands somewhere behind them, waiting. Both stalls available. They zip up, still bloated with piss, lust, trying to control their heartbeats, fight their way up for air.

He looks back at them, face tense with anticipation, as he steps up to the wall, unzips. But they are out the door without a look back, or at each other.

15

And then we are hurrying in the door and paying off the babysitter and I ache for Caroline. Can't keep from touching her, nudging her; can't wait until we're in bed, door closed, lights out. I sniff the cologne on her neck: does the babysitter notice?

We screw long and hard. Kiss until her lips are chapped from my stubble. I lick her all over: starting with her toes, up the long, smooth legs, over the bush, into the belly, savoring the tits, which seem to swell and squirm on their own. Into the armpits, down to the fingers, my tongue flicking, leaving a sticky film. Back to the bush.

"Oh," she says, over and over. "Oh."

I fondle myself until it glows purple; she does my balls. Her head is thrown back on the pillow, eyes closed, breathing heavy and raspy. So is mine. I gasp a little when one of her fingers finds my asshole and starts to massage. A little push, and part of it goes in. Hurts a little but drives me wild and I nearly come right there.

171

"I need you," I say, "I love you" and I slip it in. She is so wet that it's dripping on the sheets, and I glide into her as though she's been greased. Her hips buck up to meet mine, and we grind our pelvises together for a moment before drawing back. Back and forth, back and forth, very slowly. Sweat flowing.

"Oh," she says. "God."

Bodies slapping to a steady rhythm. The pace picks up: I'm pumping into her as fast and hard as I can. Can't control it. Autofuck. I grab her shoulders and hold on as tightly as I can.

"I'm close," I say.

"Me too."

"Say when."

"When."

It is such a feeling of relief to let it go that I nearly pass out. Flames shooting out of me, into her; she pants and makes a low gurgling sound as though she were dying. She pulls my chest against hers, pumps me as though she plans to tear it off. A long, sustained spasm of immobility. We sag against the pillows.

For a while it is impossible to say anything. then:

"Wow," she says. "You haven't been that wound up in years."

Maybe ever.

"You too," I say. "I guess the moon must be full."

"God," she says, and we drift off toward sleep for a while.

"I liked your friend," she says after a while, unexpectedly. "Brett?" Her hands stray to my dick, which is hard again. The room smells of sex, she smells of sex. She is going down on me, lightly, playfully; again the probing finger. I raise my hips a little to make it easier for her.

"He's not exactly a friend," I say. "He's just an associate at the office."

"I think he looks up to you," she says.

"Why do you say that?"

"The way he looks at you."

"He hardly knows me."

"I don't know," she says. "You must see him every day. You're what he wants to be. Where he wants to be. Successful and well thought of. You've got a family and a house. He seemed a little lonely to me."

"Brett?" I say, almost laughing. "Lonely is not the word that springs to mind. He's twenty-five, good-looking, charming. Guys like that aren't lonely."

"A ladykiller," she says absently, and returns to the business at hand. I lie back and fantasize.

I filed the petition for cert before I knew anything about Mrs. McGuire's wild tale. In a way that's a good thing, because the story would have distracted me, made me worry about how to raise the issue before the Court before I had quite figured out what it meant, and when it had not been raised in the courts below. You're not allowed to do that. It would be quite a problem if true, because Jason would then probably be found guilty of no more than some degree of manslaughter. Five years in jail, maybe, with time off for good behavior.

The Court isn't likely to review the case, in any event. This is just another death-penalty appeal, another set of desperate complaints that the trial was unfair and basic constitutional rights were violated by tiny imperfections in the proceedings. Having read a lot of these cases, I am convinced that most of the points raised in capital appeals are frivolous. Absurd. They are the frantic gasps of dying men. It is the legal equivalent of smoke inhalation. And that, I suppose, is why they must be tolerated.

Jason's case raises troubling questions even without The Story. The whole business about a juvenile being questioned without a lawyer being present, of being convicted and sentenced to death on the basis of a confession made under those circumstances is touchy stuff. In our system the state bears the burden of proving crime beyond a reasonable doubt; we can't make that burden impossible, but we can't make it too easy, either. We can't convict people and electrocute them just to satisfy the public's outrage and bloodlust. We have to do better than that.

Even if the Court denies this petition, it's just the first step in a long process of appeals. Next we go back to the circuit court in Batavia to ask for postconviction relief. If that fails, back to Criminal Appeals. If still no luck, it's on to federal district court in Monroe, petitioning for habeas corpus, if necessary appealing to the U.S. Court of Appeals for the Twelfth Circuit and the Supreme Court. There's no guarantee of success anywhere along the line, but at the least the process eats up time. It gives your client time to live. Like a doctor whose patient has a terminal illness but who successfully manages a long retreat. You lose in the end, of course, but every additional day is a victory.

The concern now is that Jason has been misdiagnosed. It is an idiotic worry.

It occurs to me, as I am shaving Monday morning, that Saturday night was not a dream, even if that's all I've been dreaming about the past few nights. It actually happened. And I actually must face the possibility of seeing Brett this morning at the office. But I won't: he works in another department, after all, for another partner, and I only seem to bump into him in the gym. No workouts today.

It can't have happened. It didn't happen. I button my top button and knot my tie—one of my favorites, the yellow power tie. Italian silk. Sets off the blue suit nicely.

"Good morning," says Caroline as I enter the kitchen.

"Good morning," I say. I sit down and glance at the Monroe paper (PROPERTY TAX HIKE LOOMS) and have some orange juice and coffee and toast. Later on, at the office, Maggie will give me what I *really* want. Doughnuts.

"Did you hear Jessie crying last night?" she says.

"No. Was she crying?"

"Yes," Caroline says. "I had to get up and change her at four."

"I didn't hear a thing."

"You were sleeping like a rock," she says. "*And* talking in your sleep."

"I was?" I say. "No I wasn't."

"You were," she says.

"What did I say?"

"I couldn't understand it," she admits. "It was mostly gobbledygook. Office talk, I guess."

"And I thought I only snored," I say.

"That, too," she says.

"I'm sorry," I say. "Maybe you should take a nap."

"I plan to try," she says.

I leave a few minutes later.

Maggie has anticipated my pleasure: there is a bag of fresh doughnuts sitting on my desk. Two chocolate glaze and one cinnamon roll. Also hot coffee.

"I'm starved," I say. "How did you know?"

"It's a Monday morning in February," she says. "I put the mail on your desk."

Ah, the mail: Mostly crap about computer software for lawyers. Bar journals, legal newspapers, information about court dates. Very occasionally a personal note from an old law-school friend who's gone off to St. Louis or Atlanta or somewhere to make a fortune.

Love it here, they say, but miss Monroe. I feel like the parent whose children have all fled the nest. You never give up the faint hope that they'll come back to this blessed place, but despite their wistful words you know they won't. They're off in some other part of the world, and the part of your life they inhabited is over. Mostly I accept that, am even glad of it sometimes—law school isn't a happy time for most people, not a well of sentimental memories—but when the little notes arrive, handwritten on the grand letterhead stationery of some law firm, I feel a little tug.

Here is a letter, but it's not on grand law-firm stationery. It's not about missing Monroe, either. I read it and feel my blood pressure rising. I pick up the phone, wanting to call him, tell him to buzz off and stop being such a manipulative little prick. But of course I don't know what number to dial, because there isn't one.

Write him a letter back. Explain, clearly, rationally, why I won't be coming to see him anymore. Why I will continue to do everything I can for him legally but will no longer subject myself to his noxious personality. Write him a Dear Jason letter, I joke to myself. It's over between us.

Dear Jason, I write on my typewriter,

Thank you for your letter. You did make me angry at my last visit. What is more important is that you've upset me at every other visit I've made to you. It's your right to be difficult and deceitful and manipulative. But don't expect that, on a personal level, I will tolerate it. I can't and I won't.

Although I have no plans to visit you again, please be assured that I will do everything possible to press your legal appeals. I believe that the criminal-justice system has seriously miscarried in your case, and, regardless of my feelings about you, I intend to see that those errors are set right.

I am glad you do not hate your mother.

> Best regards,
> Bryan Delafield

I type out an envelope and put the letter in it. Usually I like to let things sit for a while to ripen; then in an hour or two I go back and read them again to make sure they sound right. But this time I seal the letter up and put it on the outgoing pile. Get it over with. If you read it again, you won't send it. Harsh, yes, but says things that need to be said, that the kid ought to hear.

Part of me needs to be cruel.

For lunch I go out with Jack Bartlett, the senior partner, and the corporation counsel of the Grisham Company. Grisham builds buildings around Monroe; a year ago the roof of one of them fell in during a snowstorm. It was night so no one got hurt, but the property damage was extensive and the lawsuit asks for damages of several million dollars, including punitives. Grisham screwed up, no question, but the storm was uncommonly heavy—a once-in-a-hundred-years storm, say the meteorologists—and there is also good evidence that some of the materials supplied to the Grisham workers were defective. Rotted wood, mostly. In Columbia a primary contractor like Grisham is responsible for these sorts of mishaps, even if the problem can be traced to a subcontractor or supplier of material. But even if Grisham can't escape liability, we can drag in the supplier as a third-party defendant and make him pay.

The matter is embarrassing for everyone concerned and it will no doubt be settled. But like all negotiations, the lawyers on both sides have to appear to be ready to go to trial—in fact have to be ready to go to trial—in order to make possible the forging of a settlement. Like iron, parties to a lawsuit of this size usually don't start to soften until things get really hot.

We talk a lot over our steaks, briefing Grisham's in-house lawyer on the progress of discovery, the taking of the depositions, the weighing of the evidence and the legal strategies they might support, and so on. Luckily I know it all by heart, because in the back of my mind float two faces I can't make go away. The temptation is strong to have a drink or two, but I resist.

By four thirty I'm feeling relieved, proud of myself, in fact. It's been a productive day with a good lunch on somebody else, and I've not run into Brett. Not until I go to the water cooler on the next floor and there he is, filling a Mickey Mouse coffee cup. I pause, almost turn around. There is another cooler two floors up. I can get away without him ever seeing me.

But he turns around as I am thinking what to do and smiles and comes toward me. I nod.

"Hey, Bryan, how you doin'?" he says, and gives me a little punch in the upper arm.

"Hi," I say.

That's all. He is gone before we can say anything else to each other. No chitchat, sports talk, office news, nothing.

As soon as he disappears around the corner, phrases of the conversation that wasn't begin to well up in my mind.

Did you like the play?

Boy, we really got drunk. I hardly remember a thing. I was up all night peeing.

How's Peter? Did you tell him he missed all the fun?

Are you working out tonight?

I am standing there, motionless, as though I'm in a trance, when one of the secretaries comes up and asks if I'm all right. I'm fine, I say. Thank you.

I go to the fountain and get a drink of water.

What did I expect him to do? Be nice? Chat me up? Perhaps he's afraid that I'm no longer an ally in his campaign to become a partner. Partners have to know how to behave.

It occurs to me, as I ponder his glancing cruelty, that I simply don't know what's going on, that I'm rushing to conclusions. Maybe he was just in a hurry, on his way to court or to see a client.

It occurs to me that he's not giving me a chance. He's just cutting me off, deliberately, the little brat.

And am I doing the same? To send that note to Jason is to do what Brett has just done to me. I hurry back to the office to intercept the letter before it goes out. It made me feel better to write it, true, but it is full of cold nastiness from deep inside me, and he's only a kid sitting there all alone, waiting to be killed, and how could I have written him such a thing, and proposed to *send* it, when he clearly has no means of coping? The act of sending is far crueler than the words themselves.

But the "out" box is empty; the mail has already gone.

16

Caroline is sitting in a chair by the fire, trying to teach Morton Kondracke not to bite her hand or chew up everything in the house. Jessie is lying on the floor; she and Dawn are batting a whiffle ball back and forth between them. On the TV screen is "The McLaughlin Group." Caroline hopes that Morton will recognize his name when John McLaughlin says, "Mort, what do you make of this?" but the puppy is indifferent to everything but her fingers. Certainly he has no opinion on the contras, or the President's squabbling with Congress.

"Stop it," she says. "Knock it off, Mort. No biting." He wags his tail and barks at her and she has to stop herself from smiling. Or popping him one on the nose.

Bryan is at the downtown Y playing squash with Grisham's in-house lawyer. The man is nervous about the size of the suit, the unwillingness of the plaintiffs to settle—they've already been offered $250,000—and "he needs to be stroked," Bryan told her as he headed for the garage.

Outside it is snowing, and she can't help but worry about him, as she always does, when the weather is bad. His absence from a scene like this is conspicuous in her mind: fireplace, daughter, pets, a snowy night outside. Only Daddy is missing. Just like *The Homecoming* with Patricia Neal. Then the phone rings, and she knows he's calling to tell her he's going to be late, the guy wants to go out for a drink, you know I'd rather not, I'm sorry.

What can I do? he says. He represents a major client. I'm sure it won't be long. But it will be long after Jessie's bedtime.

"Hello?" she says.

"Hello," says an unfamiliar voice, deep and flat. Not one of Bryan's lawyer friends, she thinks, not that charming Brett, with his mellifluous baritone and well-turned phrases. So elegant for a man of twenty-five. She carries a vivid picture of him in her mind. No, not him; but who, then? "Is Bryan there?"

"No, I'm sorry, he isn't," she says. "Is there a message?"

"No," says the voice. "When will he be back?"

"I really don't know," she says. "I expect him at any time. Shall I tell him who's calling?"

"I don't know. OK. Just say Jason called."

Jason? Not *the* Jason, surely.

"All right, Jason, he'll know who you are, then?"

"Yeah."

"Is there a number he can reach you?"

"No number."

"Forgive me for asking," Caroline says, feeling a bit unsteady, but determined, "but are you the Jason whose appeals my husband is handling? Jason McGuire?"

"Yeah," says the voice, brightening a little and sounding, abruptly, much younger. "You know who I am?"

"Of course," Caroline says. "We've talked a lot about you, Bryan and I."

"I've seen your picture," he says. "He showed it to me."
A pause. "I should go."

"No wait," Caroline says. "Please don't. I mean, can you talk for a few minutes?"

"I don't know," says the boy. The phone is muffled for a moment before he says, "I guess so."

"Bryan's doing everything he can for you," she says. "I want you to know that. And I'm on your side. I think the death penalty is just flat wrong."

"He's mad at me," Jason says. "He won't come to see me anymore."

"Nonsense. What do you mean?"

"He just hates me," Jason says. "He was the only person who ever came to see me. I'm going to miss him," he continues, his voice shaky now.

"You're wrong," Caroline hears herself saying. "He cares very much about you. He'll be up there to see you if I have to drag him myself."

Just then there is a rattling at the door to the garage. Mort goes wild, barks, wags tail; blasts off toward the source of the disturbance. He knows what it is.

"Bye-bye," says John McLaughlin on the television.

"Jason, if you can hang on just a minute, I think Bryan has just walked in the door." She darts out to the kitchen, where Bryan is petting the puppy, and says, "Jason's on the phone and he needs to speak to you right away."

"Emergency?" Bryan says. "I'll take it in the study."

"I think so," Caroline says. "I'm not sure."

Bryan races up the stairs to the study. He locks the door and picks up the telephone, waits for the click that means Caroline has hung up.

Click.

"Hello?" he says. "Jason."

"I got your letter," Jason says. "About your not coming to visit anymore."

Bryan sighs. "Man, I am sorry about that. I wrote you another one, but I guess it hasn't gotten there yet. Why are they letting you make a phone call?"

"I let three of the guards gangbang me," he says. "You don't have to feed me that shit, you know. About the other letter and shit. There isn't another letter."

"You're right," Bryan admits. There had been thoughts of another letter, more conciliatory, upbeat, but it did not get written. The feeling wasn't there. But how will it be possible to explain that?

"So you admit you just fuckin' lied," Jason says. "After you bitched me out for lying."

"I'm sorry."

"Yeah, well I'm sorry too. I call up to tell you how sorry I am, I get myself reamed up the ass four times in an hour just so I can get to the goddamn telephone, and you're lying to me right off the bat. You stinking bastard."

"Jason, this is pointless," Bryan says. "If anything develops I'll let you know."

"Don't hang up on me!" he shouts. "Please!"

But Bryan does.

"You what?" Caroline says.

"I had to," Bryan says. "It was just going to be another shouting match."

"I don't understand," she says slowly, "what all the quarreling is about."

"Neither do I," Bryan says. "But it always happens and nothing good comes out of it. It's better if I don't have anything to do with him personally. It was a mistake ever to go there in the first place. Lay eyes on the little thug."

"He told me you're the only person who ever visits him."

"He told me that, too. I'm not sure I believe him."

"You can't just leave him there all by himself. He needs some human contact. God knows what's happening to him there. Everybody knows what goes on in prisons."

Bryan says nothing.

"He can't just be left there with no contact to the outside world," she says, Monrovian indignation flaring. "I mean it. I'll go visit him myself if that's what it takes."

"Don't be ridiculous," he says. "You're making way too much of this. My job is to handle his appeals, not to babysit him or be his buddy. And your job is to butt out."

"That's bullshit," she says. "If you really believe that, then you're not the lawyer I thought you were. Or the man."

"Caroline, why are we fighting?"

"Because here's a kid on death row, no contact with the world, nobody cares about him and he knows it, he's your client, someone who depends on you, his whole life, you're all he's got, and you're hanging up the phone on him. You won't go visit him."

"You're the one," he says slowly, "who was always pouting when I said I had to go see him."

"I was wrong," she says. "I didn't understand what it meant to him. I wasn't thinking clearly about his situation."

"I don't think you know anything about his situation. I don't think you really know anything about him. What he's like. I do."

"I talked to him tonight," she says. "Before you came in. I listened to his voice, Bryan. He's just a kid. He misses you."

"The kid is a cold-blooded killer."

"You really don't believe the mother's story?"

"No," he says.

Neither of them are convinced.

"I think I do," she says. "I think you've got to find out."

"Hey," Bryan says. "This is my case and I'll handle it the way I see fit."

"It isn't just your case," she says. "It's our case. It affects us. It affects you. It's not good for you to turn to stone on someone like this who needs help, when you know he needs you and I know you care about him. You need to go more with your feelings."

"I don't know why you think I care about him," he says. "That's a silly thing to say. I've already let my feelings carry me too far in this case. They're all guilty, let's face it. They know what the law is. Let them fry. Lawyers have better things to do than defend degenerates."

"I can't believe you."

"Well, I'm sorry," he says, more gently. "It's just that this whole thing has been such a drag, and I never expected it. I mean, I thought I was going to be arguing about the Fifth and Sixth Amendments. They never told me all the rest was going to happen. I don't want to deal with this but it's all I think about."

"He's your client," she says. "It's that simple. You can't just cut the boy off, even if he is obnoxious and difficult. He's one lonely, desperate boy, Bryan. In trouble we can't even imagine. It's just not right to pretend he isn't there."

He feels an enormous pressure to resist her easy idealisms. Truly she does not understand what it is with Jason. She does not understand how dangerous he is, even in prison, chained and handcuffed, stored behind bars: she does not understand how he is able to roil his emotions so they seem beyond his control. That is not a feeling he likes, and he instinctively shies away.

She does not understand the limits he sees as his duty to Jason: his obligations, professional and personal. It is not his job to be the kid's friend. It is not his job to soothe the kid's troubled soul. It is his job to represent Jason in the legal system and, in the process, make the system work the way it's supposed to.

But that's simplistic, too. No lawyer can completely disengage his emotions from a case like this. Lawyers do more than write briefs and make motions; representing a client is more than that. It is understanding the client, knowing the client, looking out for the client's best interests. Comforting the client, if that's what's needed. He knows it. He's done it.

And the nagging doubt. He does not really want to know the truth. It shouldn't matter. But it does, to justice and to his own feelings, and he knows that he must find out.

"All right," he sighs, "so what am I supposed to do?"

"You have to go see him," she says without hesitation. "You have to let him know he's got a friend, and you have to find out if the story's true, if you can. That makes a difference, doesn't it? That changes everything, doesn't it?"

"I've tried."

"Try again."

"I don't know."

"I'll come if you want. I'd like to meet him."

"You can't," he says. "Attorney-client privilege. And we're talking about a prison here." And, he does not add aloud, I just don't want you there. This is between him and me.

It's no easy matter to arrange to see Jason in a setting other than that ghastly little conference room. I speak to the warden. I speak to the head of the Department of Corrections. I am almost certain he's going to tell me I need to talk to the governor, but instead he sends me back to the warden, a man named Riley. Taciturn, abrupt but not unfriendly: I don't exactly envy him his job. He's the one who has to stand there at each execution and ask the condemned for his or her last words. He's the one who has to nod to the little ghoul in the operating booth: Throw the switch. He's the one who has to meet the press afterward to describe how things went, what the last meal was, what the condemned's state of mind was, and so forth. And he does this all the time—at least that's the way it's seemed in Columbia the past few years. I have to remind myself that I'm in favor of this institution. I am. It's nasty business, wrapped in a horrible shroud of medievalism, but necessary. It's not the warden's fault.

"Well, Mr. Delafield, I guess I'm not exactly sure what you want," said Warden Riley when I called him back. "I ain't runnin' a boys' school here."

"I'm quite aware of that, Warden. What I'd like to do basically, if this is possible, is just to spend some time alone with my client. A day, if that's possible, maybe two, and somewhere other than in that conference room. He's very young, as you know, and he needs to relax in order to talk to me more fully."

"I've seen 'em a lot younger," the Warden said shortly, telegraphing his position on the matter. "Don't quite know what I can do to help you, Mr. Delafield. Only place you could really be alone with the boy would be in one of them trailers we keep for the wives."

The conjugal-visit trailers. Perfect, but I could hear his silent snicker over the phone line from a hundred miles away.

"Would that be possible?" I said with as much dignity as I could muster. "That would be perfect."

"Well, 'course, you ain't married to him, are you?" said the Warden. "Death-row inmates don't have conjugal rights anyway."

"This is an emergency," I said. "Please, Warden. I need to spend some time alone with Jason McGuire. His whole case could depend on it."

"Ain't got much of a case, from what I understand," said Riley. Pause. "What the hell. Don't bother me none, if we got one available. You'll have to get approval from the Department of Corrections. You understand, don't you, Mr. Delafield, that these trailers are on the prison grounds proper?"

"Yes."

"And that guards are around at all times and can come in at any time, without saying anything?"

"I do."

"*Any* time?"

"Warden," I said, "I'll have the Department call you within the hour to OK this."

"OK," he said. "Fine by me."

And so, on a Saturday morning the last day in February, I am once again speeding down the highway toward Warrensville. My overnight bag is in the back seat. I will be home for Sunday supper. Caroline understands. I'm the one who doesn't understand. Not yet.

PART III
ENDINGS

17

The scene: a battered mobile home lying in permanent state on a bier of concrete bricks. The trailer a giant shoebox made of steel sheets painted a mournful yellow, as though afflicted by hepatitis.

A number of these forlorn structures are clustered together in a little shantytown a few hundred yards from the main cell blocks. The ground around them is bare; a few weeds grow in summer, nothing but dirty snow in winter. No trees. A few picnic tables; the skeleton of an umbrella. A football low on air.

It is here that prisoners meet their wives and loved ones, spend a few hours, a day or two alone with them. It is in these shabby little cans that the world of prison intersects with the world outside. Where it is possible—if that is a good thing—for a prisoner to be reminded exactly what's out there, and how different that is from what's inside.

Bryan sits uncomfortably on the sofa in what he supposes is the living room. The walls are covered by plastic paneling done up to look like mahogany or walnut: hard to tell which, if either. A few pale watercolors in battered frames. The smell of rotting carpet, cigarette smoke, beer. The scents of desperate couples.

Elsewhere in the trailer is a bedroom and a bath with a mildewed shower. The living room gives into a little dining area and then a small kitchen with an electric range. Motley bits of furniture here and there: a chair with uneven legs, a scratched table, a lamp with no shade. Like a low-rent whorehouse.

He has been waiting here twenty minutes, ever since the guards brought him from the warden's office. Two of them are still waiting outside, waiting for Jason to be brought from his cell. They are smoking cigarettes and talking; he can hear their voices through the thin sheet metal of the walls.

Guards will be close at hand at all times, he has been told repeatedly, and can make unannounced searches at any time. The warden still seems perplexed by the arrangement, faintly hostile even, and that attitude is strongly reflected in the guards, who have no idea what's going on but dislike it nonetheless. They are trained to dislike, hired for it, professional at it.

He hasn't been made to wait like this, made so nervous, since Jessie was born. It's odd, he thinks, how alike prisons and hospitals are. Everything regimented, grim: nobody will tell you anything. Everybody seems to be waiting for something. The inhuman smells. He squirms in discomfort.

The front door swings open and a guard troops in with a bag full of groceries from the prison commissary.

"Know how to cook, pal?" the guard says.

"We'll manage."

The guard takes the food into the kitchen and sets the bag down on the counter.

"Your little murderer friend'll be along any minute," says the guard. "I think they're givin' him one last strip-search." He gives Bryan a lewd wink.

"Thank you," Bryan says.

"Sure thing," says the guard, and tromps back out into the dirty snow.

And there are more footsteps at the front door.

"I thought you'd had it with me," Jason says. "I thought you'd never come to see me again."

"I didn't think I would, either," Bryan says.

They are sitting in the living room, in the two tattered easy chairs, watching a gray snow fall on the heads of the guards just outside the window. There is wariness in the air, uncertainty between them.

"Are you hungry?" Bryan says.

"Not really."

"Because they brought some food. We could have soup or something."

"Maybe later."

Pause.

"So why did you come back?"

"I had to find out," Bryan says simply. "About your dad and your brother. Whether it is true."

"We fought about that the last time."

"I know," Bryan says. "This time let's just talk about it."

"I don't know what she told you."

"She said"—he takes a deep breath—"that they were both, ah, abusing you. Taking liberties. You know. That's what she thought. She never actually saw anything and nobody told her anything. But she seemed sure it was true."

"It is true," Jason says simply. "They fucked the shit out of me."

Bryan gets up for some crackers and cheese.

"I don't understand."

"I don't, either, really," Jason admits. "I hated them."

"Why didn't you just tell them to knock it off?" Bryan asks. "Why didn't you just push them off you? Why didn't you just kick them or something?"

"They would have hurt me," Jason said. "They told me so. They said they'd tell everyone that I was a queer and a faggot and that I asked to suck them off every night."

"Oh man," Bryan says. "Why didn't you tell this to your lawyer for the trial?"

"No way, man."

"They probably wouldn't have even convicted you. Let alone give you the sentence they did."

Jason shakes his head. No way.

An early dinner of chicken soup and cheese sandwiches. Bryan warms the soup, Jason makes the sandwiches. They put everything on plates and take it back to the living room, where they sit together on the couch, in front of the portable black-and-white TV Bryan has brought for the slower moments.

One of the guards bursts in during the middle of an "All in the Family" rerun. He looks around, looks at them, shouts something to a comrade outside.

"Hey," he says.

"Hey," Bryan says.

"Just checking."
"We're fine."
The guard leaves.
"Well," Bryan says, "that wasn't so bad."
"Wait till they come in in the middle of the night."
"They do that?"
"They do anything they want."

The guard made me feel naked, and after he leaves we sit there for a while watching the television but not really paying attention. Jason is slumped down on my right, not saying a thing; the sneering is gone, the malice gone, that horrible smile. He hardly seems to be there at all. I can't think of anything to say. All I can think of is that I'm sitting here alone with a murderer in a shabby little trailer in the middle of a prison in the middle of the winter. Guards and spotlights all over the place. It feels like a black-and-white movie. Desperate hours: Bogie. I wish that one of us would say something.

"You want to play chess?" I ask. "I brought my little set."

"Don't know how."

It's fun, I tell him. Kind of like a war: strategy, battles, psychological games. Okay, he says, why not? I set up the board and tell him about the game's basic rules, principles.

I get it, he says. Let's play.

We play, and I checkmate him in three moves: a plan of attack I learned in college. I'm afraid he'll be angry or frustrated, but he wants to play again. I try the same opening gambit, but he is alert, and for a moment actually takes advantage of the fact that my queen is out of position to attack my king. I must scramble a bit to recover.

"Funny thing," he says suddenly, during a lull in the

action, while I am pondering what to do with an errant knight, "sometimes I liked it."

"When they fucked you?" It is a shock to hear these words spring from my lips. I am talking to a kid, after all.

"Yeah," he says. "I'm not sure, you know, but sometimes I, like—" He makes a tiny milking gesture with his hand. I get it. I nod.

"While . . . you know. It was happening. Sometimes after. That's pretty bad, isn't it?"

"Jason," I say, "I don't know."

"It's not like I'm queer or anything."

"I know that," I say. "But if you liked it then why did you kill them?"

"Because I hated them," he says. "Because they raped me. It hurt. They were rough. It wasn't like they were doing it because they loved me or anything. It's not like I wanted them to love me or anything," he continues, a little frantically, "I mean, nothing that queer. I can't explain. I didn't say I liked it. I said sometimes I liked it."

"Do you have something against queers?"

"Not really," he says. "I'm just not one."

"Me neither."

That's settled.

"Check," he says, and I get up to take the dishes into the kitchen.

"Tell me a story."

"What kind of story?"

"How you met your wife."

"Why do you want to know about that?"

"I just do."

Night now. He is curled up like a ball at one end of the old sofa. I lounge at the other. A guard was in here about half an hour ago, poking around like a bear in a garbage dump. Nothing for him to find. The chessboard is where we left it some hours ago, the pieces arranged inconclusively. He picked the game up amazingly fast.

"Well," I begin, and as I do so he shifts his body so that the top of his head is pushed up against the outside of my right thigh. Jessie does the same thing. The warmth is pleasant; the trailer drafty. "I was in law school, and she worked in the library. I guess I was about twenty-five and she was twenty-one or so."

"Did you have girlfriends before?"

"Not really," I say. "School, you know. Always a lot of homework. I didn't have a lot of social experience."

"You don't look like a nerd."

"Thanks," I say. "Good to know."

"I never had a girlfriend," he says. "Patrick did."

"Yes?" I say. "Was he serious about them?"

"What do you mean?"

"I mean, you know, physically."

"I don't know. I doubt it." Why else, he doesn't need to say, would he have been so eager to have me? "They might have given him hand jobs or something. I never knew for sure."

"Did you like Patrick?"

"Oh, yeah," Jason says. "He was a great brother."

"Are you sorry he's gone?"

"Sometimes. Sometimes I don't even believe this whole thing is real. I think I'm dreaming and some day I'll just wake up and it'll be summer and no school. You know?"

"Yes." The smell of honeysuckle; carefree days. Roasting marshmallows on the grill, playing in the vacant lot at the end of the block. I know.

"Do you love her?" he says. "Your wife?"

"Sure," I say, reverie interrupted.

"Totally hot for her?"

"I'm not sure that's any of your business," I say, "but yes."

"Ever fool around on her?"

"Jason, what the hell are we talking about here?"

"I don't know. I guess that means you have."

"I don't think that's any of your business."

"You have."

"I was too shy to talk to her," I say, continuing with the saga of Caroline, "so she talked to me. I needed some book from behind the desk—that's where she was working nights—and she just started to chat me up."

"Did you sleep with her right away?"

"You're sure nosey."

"You were a virgin."

Pause.

"Yes," I say softly. "More or less. How did you know?"

"What does that mean, more or less?"

"I had a few close calls in college," I say dismissively, "but none of them amounted to anything."

"What's it like?" he says. "Screwing a girl?"

"It's hard to describe," I say cautiously.

"Like screwing a guy?"

"How would I know?"

"You've never screwed a guy?"

"Most guys don't screw other guys," I say.

"So you've never fooled around with another guy?"

I say nothing.

"Does she know?" he asks.

I shake my head.

The boy has gone off to bed, and Bryan is watching the late news on the little TV. Thinking. Thinking about what

Jason has told him, what he has confirmed. So it's all true: he believed it all along, didn't believe it. Could never quite decide. Of course it's possible the kid is lying, but the mood today has been one of candor, and he knows, feels for certain, that this time Jason is telling the truth.

Telling the truth, guessing the truth: The boy is disconcertingly shrewd. How has he guessed? Does he know? Where it happened? Caroline stopped all that. She was all he needed. He can't possibly know.

On the screen is a man with a microphone standing in front of a sign that says "Columbia State Prison." The man says, "Final preparations are being made for the execution of convicted killer Phillip Masterson, who is scheduled to die in the electric chair here shortly after midnight tonight. Masterson was sentenced for killing his mother as part of an insurance scam seven years ago. His lawyers are meeting with the governor in Monroe at this hour, asking for a grant of clemency . . ."

It's funny, he thinks, not paying much attention to the television, it wouldn't have mattered what I said to him, how much I denied doing those things. He knew anyway. He is dangerous. The weather forecast is next. After that, try to sleep.

Bryan awakens sometime later, television still on, to the sound of shuffling feet. At first he thinks it is one of the guards come to check things out, but when his eyes open he sees Jason standing there, trembling, dressed only in white jockey shorts.

"It's midnight," he says.

"Why aren't you asleep?"

"They're doing it to Phillip right now."

"Who's Phillip?"

"A guy."

"He's being executed tonight?"

"Right now," Jason says. He shivers again.

"How do you know?"

"I just do."

"Put some clothes on," Bryan says. "You'll freeze. Here." He hands him one of the sweaters he brought along, and Jason slips it on. "This Phillip, he's a friend of yours?"

"I know him." He goes to a window and looks out at the cell blocks, the other prison buildings. A few lights are on here and there, but mostly it's quiet, dark. Bryan joins Jason at the window and slips an arm around his shoulder.

"You can't see anything from here," he says. "Why don't you get back into bed? At least it's warm there. We'll talk in the morning."

"I can't sleep," Jason says. "I can't sleep on nights like this. I never do." He is shivering harder now, despite the sweater, and Bryan takes the boy in his arms and rocks him gently.

"Easy, easy," he says. "Take it easy. Let's go back to bed." He starts to lead Jason toward the bedroom.

"Please," Jason says, "can I stay out here with you for a while?"

"Sure," Bryan says, "sure. If that's what you want." He goes into the bedroom and brings out the blanket Jason had been lying under. They settle in on the couch, TV still on. Jason snuggles under Bryan's arm.

"I'm glad you're here," he says in a small voice. "I feel safe."

"I'm glad, too," he says, and they doze off, indifferent for a while to the guards, to Phillip's date with Gretchen, to the world outside.

Bang goes the door in the middle of the night. A blast of cold air, shattered light from a search lamp somewhere off in the yard: a guard stomps in. He throws the light switch in the living room.

"Hey," he says in a conversational tone, "the little faggot is doing his lawyer." He comes over to the sofa, where Jason has fallen asleep in the crook of Bryan's arm, and Bryan has himself dozed off, but they are awake before he has a chance to shake them.

"What are you doing?" Bryan says.

"What are *you* doing?" the guard says.

"We were sound asleep," Bryan says. "There's no problem here. Please leave."

"All balled up on the couch together," says the guard. "Ain't that cute."

"Phillip," Jason says in a weak voice.

"Dead as a doornail. He won't be fuckin' you no more. But I guess that don't matter if you got your lawyer pal here to do it for you."

Bryan is unaware of his arm tightening around Jason's shoulder, of the overtly protective gesture he has assumed.

"I understand," he says, "that you have the right to come in here anytime, unannounced. I understood that when I came here. But you had better understand that you can't just do anything you want or say anything you want. This is harassment."

"You givin' me lip, queer?" the guard says. "Maybe you'd like to do me too."

"He's drunk," Jason whispers to Bryan. "He is a lot."

The guard has unzipped his fly and is waving his penis at them.

"Which one of you nelly boys wants a piece of this baby?" he says. "I know you do," he says to Jason. "Wouldn't be the first time. How 'bout you, Mr. Lawyer? Bet you never laid your hands on one this big."

"Jake, how's your wife?" Jason says.

"None of your fuckin' business, you little queer!" he spits, and the penis, which had shown signs of expansion, wilts. "My fuckin' wife," he says furiously, to the wall. "My fuckin' bitch wife. Bitch." He says it again, looks at them speculatively over his shoulder. "Got a wife, queer boy?"

"Yes," Bryan says. Jason can feel his muscles tensing, knows he wants to get up and slug the man. But Jason holds him tighter, and he doesn't get up from the couch.

"She know you're sacked out here with this little killer fruit?"

"As a matter of fact, yes."

"Must be a fuckin' lezzie," he says absently, and after a burp wanders back out into the night, leaving the door open. Jason waits several long moments to be sure he is gone, then darts over to close out the night and the cold. By the time he is back under Bryan's arm he's shivering.

"Are all the guards like that?" Bryan asks. "That abusive?"

"Not all of them. Hardly any, in fact. Most of them are OK."

"What did he mean, this wouldn't be the first time you'd . . . you know."

"Man, they can do anything they want," Jason says, "and there's nothing you or anybody else can do about it. I can live with it. Don't worry."

"Why you?"

"I'm pretty," he says. "Don't you know anything?"

"I thought people were always locked up."

"That just means you can't get away when they come for you."

"Look. If these guards are raping you, your constitutional rights are being violated. Right and left. We'll sue the hell out of them."

"No way, man," Jason says. "That's the last thing we're going to do. Let's go to sleep."

But, Bryan protests silently, but there must be a way to win. He falls asleep trying to think of it.

At breakfast Jason asks, "Did it bother you last night when that guy called you a queer?"

"Not really," I say. "No."

"He meant it, you know. He thinks I'm a queer."

"And you're not."

"'Course I'm not," Jason says. "Fuck you."

"Don't get mad," I say. "It's just that we've never really talked about it."

"You a queer?"

"No," I say slowly.

"Fuck, man," Jason says, "you told me last night you made it with guys."

"I never said that."

"You didn't say you didn't."

"I was being honest with you. I was drunk. I hardly knew it was happening."

"And I'm locked up in a cell, waiting to get fried or until somebody barges in to fuck my brains out in the meantime. That make me queer?"

"Jason, I never said you were queer. Never thought so. I was just wondering whether you ever thought so."

"I am not a fuckin' queer, man," he says. "And if you say it again you might as well get the fuck out of here 'cause you won't be my lawyer anymore."

"You still haven't told me," I say, "why you didn't tell Edwards about your brother and father. He could have used that at trial. It would have changed everything."

"You mean if I'd gone up there and talked about it," Jason says. "That's what you mean."

"Yes."

"Let the whole fuckin' world know that I'm getting it every night like a girl from my brother and my dad. Tell them that."

"If that's what happened to you, if that's why you felt you had to kill them, then yes."

"Get a clue."

"Don't you see?" I say. "Can't you see that it doesn't make you a queer that your father and brother were molesting you? It wasn't your fault. They did it to you."

"I let them," Jason says. "I liked it."

"But that's not the point. They started it. They perpetuated it. They did it."

"Fuck."

Silence. We eat our cornflakes and drink our orange juice.

"I'd like to try to bring this up somehow," I say after a while. "Try to get you a new trial or something. Maybe we can say that Edwards was incompetent or that all the relevant evidence wasn't introduced." I don't mention how difficult this will be: It was Jason who withheld the evidence that might have helped him, and it will be difficult for a court to give him, in effect, a second chance. There's always the governor, however, and the untold story might well move him to clemency. Stranger things have happened. "It will get you out of here."

"Forget it, man."

"Why?"

"I've told you why. Just forget it."

"But Jason," I say, "you're cutting your own throat."

"My throat to cut."

Instinctively I reach across the table and take his hand. "All I want," I say, "is to get you out of here."

"Then do it," he says, and he is once again the chilly, inscrutable boy I first met almost a year ago. Except he does not let go of my hand.

"I will," I say.

In the Supreme Court of the United States

Jason Lee McGuire, Petitioner
v.
State of Coumbia, Respondent.
No. CR-6894
Petition for Certiorari to the
Columbia Court of Criminal Appeals
May 27.

The petition for a writ of certiorari is DENIED.

Justice WASHINGTON, with whom Justices BECKER and HOWARD join, dissenting:

We would grant the petition for certiorari and vacate the judgment below insofar as it leaves undisturbed the sentence of death imposed upon petitioner.

18

WASHINGTON (AP)—The Supreme Court today refused to review the case of Jason Lee McGuire, a Batavia, Columbia, man who was convicted and sentenced to death for murdering his father and brother while he was still a teenager. The vote was 6-3, with Justice Louise Washington's dissenting statement joined by Justices Frank Becker and Jane Howard.

"Of course I'm extremely disappointed," said McGuire's lawyer, Bryan Delafield of Monroe. "There are serious constitutional problems in this case."

But, he added, "we will press on with our postconviction appeals and, if necessary, seek habeas corpus in federal court. I'm confident that we'll succeed at some point."

Supporters of the death penalty hailed the Court's action.

"It shows they implicitly recognize that you shouldn't be immune from the death penalty just because you're young," said Sandra Byers, assistant attorney general of Columbia. "You can't just bring any old appeal any more and expect them to listen to it."

McGuire was convicted and sentenced to death last

January for the murders of Donald McGuire, 51, and Patrick McGuire, 18, both of Batavia. The two men were knifed to death in their sleep. McGuire is the youngest person on Columbia's death row and the only person in this century sentenced to death by a Columbia jury for a crime he committed as a juvenile. No execution date has been set.

The news comes by telephone from the firm's D.C. office, while Bryan is down the hall getting coffee. Maggie hands him the call memo slip without saying anything. She knows as well as he does what it means. He goes in and makes the call and gets the confirmation. Some papers are already on their way via Federal Express.

"Fuck," he says to an empty office. He leans back in his chair and looks out the window at the state capitol. It would have been his first chance to argue in the Supreme Court. To stand at that lectern and show his stuff. To field the justices' questions, let them know he was a force to be reckoned with.

If only they knew, he thinks, but of course they don't. All they have to go by is the written record of the case, the confession, the trial transcript, the decision of the Court of Criminal Appeals. They do not know, have no way of knowing, what actually happened. Why he did it. Knowing virtually nothing of the truth of the case, how can they possibly render justice? And yet there is no appeal from their decision. They hold the last word on Jason, and they have no clue.

The coffee tastes bitter this morning.

Brett is hanging around the coffee machine long after everyone else in the office, in the whole building, has gone home for the night. The sports page obscures his face, but he lowers the paper when Bryan emerges from his office, overcoat in one hand, briefcase in the other.

"Hey man," he says. "You're here late."

"You too."

For a moment it appears that this conversation, like their last one, will wither on the vine of embarrassment after a halting word or two. But Brett rallies unexpectedly.

"Checkin' out the sports," he says with a laugh, waving the newsprint like a fan. Bryan does not laugh. Brett clears his throat and goes on: "I heard about your appeal for that kid. Tough bounce."

"Not unexpected," says Bryan, more stiffly than he intends. "And given the record we probably would have lost anyway even if they'd taken it. Case isn't a winner on paper."

"You ever get the scoop on him?"

"Can't say."

"Sure," Brett says.

They look at each other uncomfortably. Who will be the first to bring it up? Brett? He looks seasick. Bryan? He's scrambling to collect himself; didn't expect to find Brett here, all alone, as though waiting. He is not prepared.

"So," Brett says after an awkward moment, "you working out tonight?"

"Not tonight."

"I thought I might go down and lift some weights. I'll bet it's not crowded at all. Nobody around tonight."

"No," Bryan says. "Well, see you tomorrow."

"OK," says Brett. "I'm off." He pauses, takes a deep breath, but doesn't move. "So how's the wife and kid?"

"Fine," Bryan says. "In fact I'm on my way home to them right now. Dinner."

"I liked your wife," he says. "Caroline?"

"Right," Bryan says. "She liked you, too."

"Did she?" He seems genuinely pleased. "I'm surprised she remembers me."

"She never forgets a face."

"Well," he says, struggling a bit. Bryan is not helping. "Tell her I said hello."

"I will," Bryan says. "Good night." And he is off to the drinking fountain and out the door. Brett goes down to the gym, where the only other person around is a gaunt middle-aged man in a towel hovering near the door to the steam room. He lifts his weights quickly and leaves without taking a shower.

And, as if it isn't enough that Jessie is screaming her lungs out about something or other, Morton Kondracke has to come strolling into the living room and take a large shit in front of the fireplace.

"Oh Christ," I say. "Goddamn it, Mort." I rush over and scold him, the smell rising into my nostrils. I swat him a few times, hard, on his little butt, and he looks at me with big brown eyes and whimpers.

"What is it?" Caroline calls from Jessie's bedroom, where a diaper change is in progress.

"Mort crapped all over everything," I say. "The little fucker." I pick him up furiously and rush him into the kitchen, banish him to his little cage for the rest of the night.

"I told you he had to go out," Caroline calls. "That's why he was barking before."

"How the hell am I supposed to know that? The shit needs to be cleaned up."

"Can you do it, please?" she says in a reasonable tone that galls me. "I'm a little busy here."

"He's your goddamn dog," I say. "You do it." But the

smell is so strong that I abandon principle for a handful of paper towels, a plastic bag, and the can of deodorant.

No talking for a while. Mort's whimpers die down; Jessie is put to bed. Dawn roams the sofa cushions, looking for something to shred. Caroline reappears.

"I know you had a bad day," she says. "I'm sorry."

"A lot you know about it," I say.

"I know you're upset."

"It was a hellish day," I say, "and I come home to a madhouse that smells like shit. I am tired of hearing that baby cry, I'm tired of having that goddamn little dog shitting all over everything and whining, and I just hate it when the cat bats her ball around in the middle of the night."

I need a vacation.

"I'm sorry," Caroline says. "I don't know what we can do about it all."

"I know what I can do," I say. "I can leave."

"Leave?"

"Leave. Go to a hotel. Go on a vacation. Go anywhere but here."

"By yourself?"

"That's the whole point," I say.

"If you need to get away for a while," she says slowly, "I think I can understand that."

"I don't know," I say, "if it's just a matter of a while." This is not quite what I expected to say, and it stuns us both a little.

"I know this thing has been tough on you," she says after a moment, "but don't you think you might be losing your perspective a little? Just step back and take a deep breath and think about something else for a while."

"This thing is none of your fucking business," I say. "A lot you know about it."

"I know one thing," she says. "A lawyer who lets his professional life disrupt his personal life is a fool."

"And what about the lawyer who lets his personal life disrupt his professional life?"

"If you're suggesting that Jessie and I are making it difficult for you to practice law," she says, "then perhaps you should leave."

I nod, though I'm not at all sure that's what I was suggesting.

So I am sitting here in the Holiday Inn at two in the morning watching CNN. The sound is turned off. Can't quite believe it. I just got up and said, "Fine" and put on my coat and went to the garage and took off. It was surprisingly easy to do. Painless. It's almost a relief to be here—easier to breathe. When I got to my hotel room I stripped to my shorts and just lay down for a while, to bathe in the freedom.

Tomorrow I will call her. Tell her I'm all right. Tell her I'll be back in a little while—a few days, whatever.

The truth is that I don't really want to go back.

The stories I never told Jason—didn't have to, he seemed to know them already—were from college. About the park along Lake Monroe, right on campus. My first time—must have been a sophomore—was an accident. I was walking home from a late Saturday night at the library, a little groggy, a little depressed about something. The meaninglessness of life, I suppose. The usual stuff. Weltschmerz.

The direct route home was along University, a well-lit, well-traveled boulevard that ran the entire length of the campus and on to Monroe's west side. Full of bikers and joggers, strollers, buses, even at night. That was my accustomed route.

The scenic route was Lakeside Path, a trail that connected several small parks along the shore. I ran along it sometimes during the day, when it was like a freeway. At night it was mostly deserted—empty picnic tables, benches, a small brick rest room. I chose this route because, I thought, I wanted to think. Let me be alone to brood, ponder. Strange what your subconscious will choose for you if you let it.

May: mild, fresh, a clear night full of stars and a bright moon that shimmered on the lake. I walked along feeling very alone but enjoying the smells of spring, listening to the gentle lap of unseen waves against the shoreline. It's the prettiest time of year in Monroe; the pulse of life is strong.

Monroe Park, near the end of the path, was one of the loveliest in the city. From its sandy beach it climbed sharply away from the water onto a small wooded hill before opening into University and the comfortable old homes beyond. The hill commanded a lovely view of the capitol dome, glowing white under a black sky.

It was Wednesday, 11 P.M. The dome. Light diffused among the trees, leaves just begining to thicken. The smell of green, of damp dark earth.

Shadowy figures moving about. Back and forth. Looking. Standing. Approach, withdraw, circle. Light cigarette.

Bolt? Scream? Pray? Couldn't do any of those things. Mesmerized; paralyzed. Nausea. Dry mouth. Shivering, even though it is mild. Life. Stayed until 4 A.M., the eastern sky paling slightly. Slept until dinnertime.

Obsessed. Then Caroline. She settled the matter, quelled the thirst.

Didn't she?

So it's 3 A.M. and I'm flat on my back doing it again

because I can't get to sleep. Sometimes it helps wear you out, send you into one of those dreamless states from which you wake feeling that not a minute has passed.

Mind roaming, searching for fantasy. I think of the first time with Caroline, in the basement of her parents' home while they were away for the day. Stale: change subject. The bushes: shadows, jeans, buttons, jockeys, white; half-lighted young faces tense with concentration, pleasure, fear. Prisoners.

It does not even bother me, right now, that these are the most potent images. It's been years, I think. Something's changed, changing.

I see the face, the teeth, the eyes; feel the skin. Young, smooth, strong. It's over in twenty seconds. Still awake.

"Something's happened to you," Caroline says. We are sitting in a sunny little restaurant a few blocks from the Capitol. A man behind a glass wall is making sticky buns.

"Yes," I say vacantly. Then: "What do you mean?"

"I'm not sure, exactly," she says. "You're cold. I thought you'd at least be glad to see me after three days."

"I am."

"You are not. It's because of what I said about Jason, isn't it?"

"What did you say?"

"I said," she says slowly, as though I could possibly have forgotten, "that you were too involved with him."

"Nice choice of words," I say. "You make it sound like we're having an affair."

"Maybe that's kind of what it is," she says. "The same kind of obsession."

"What do you know about obsession? Affairs of your own?"

"Don't insult me," she says. "I came here to tell you I was sorry I'd offended you. I was hoping you'd want to come home."

"I don't want to come home," I say.

"Well," she says, and I can see she's flustered. "Take your time."

"How's Jessie?"

"Fine. She asks where you are. I tell her you had to go out of town on business."

"I'll pop in to see her soon," I say.

"How do we explain it when you don't stay?"

"We'll say I'm going away on business again. That should tide us over for a little while."

"Bryan," she says, "are we over?"

"I don't know."

"I dont' get it," she says. "It can't just be Jason. That can't be the whole thing, can it? It can't be. What's gone wrong?"

"I don't know," I say, and I don't. I leave some money for the bill and leave her in the restaurant, wondering whether she can cry, should cry, will cry. I cry.

19

Hey, says the note.

I know you think I'm wrong but I'm not. If you were me, would you tell? It's our secret.

A smear of blood at the bottom, possibly a thumbprint. This is the little piece of gray paper Bryan is clutching in his pocket as he sits in the chambers of U.S. District Judge James Flannery. Judge Flannery is fat and jolly, fond of the ribald anecdote, but a hard-liner on criminal matters and famously reluctant to intervene in capital cases. He is not an easy sell. In fact he is an impossible sell. But after the failure of the postconviction relief motions, Bryan has no choice. The governor has signed the death warrant, and an execution date has been set: less than a month from now, at the end of the month. He has no choice at all. His hands work reflexively on the note in his pocket.

"Your Honor," says Sandy Byers, "as I said in my brief, I think Mr. McGuire's motion is completely frivolous.

There's just no reason at all to grant habeas in this case. The Court of Criminal Appeals has reviewed the matter twice and found nothing out of order. I think it's an insult to the whole system, frankly, to be dragging a federal judge into this."

"Well," says the judge offhandedly, leaning back in his leather swivel chair and lighting a cigar. "Mr. Delafield, tell my why I should grant your motion."

"Your Honor," Bryan says, a little hesitantly. "I'm afraid I persist in my belief that the confession used to convict my client was illegally obtained. No lawyer was present when he was questioned."

"Oh, come off it, Counsel," says Flannery. "You've been up to bat with that old stick one time too many. If that's all you've got, then I'm going to deny your motion right now."

Sandra's expression is rigid: a mask of control. She has said all she needs to say. Bryan flushes.

"No, Your Honor," he says, "that's not all I've got."

"Good," says the judge. "Let's hear it."

"I wonder if I might speak to you privately, Your Honor," Bryan says. "I'm sure Ms. Byers won't mind."

Now Sandra looks uncomfortable, sensing a deal will be cut, man to man, while she's sitting in the waiting room reading an old *Cosmopolitan.* But:

"Afraid I can't do that, Counsel. The state is part of these proceedings. I can't very well ask its representative to leave at a time like this."

"It's a very sensitive matter, Your Honor," Bryan says. "Extremely so."

"Go ahead," Sandra says. "I'm not a virgin."

The judge frowns at her. It's the first thing she's said all morning he doesn't entirely approve of. He swivels forward, rests his elbows on his large desk. For an instant he gives every indication that he will indeed ask her to leave unless she gives a satisfactory account of her sex life.

"Mr. Delafield," he says. "Please proceed."

Bryan sits there for a moment, puzzling. It would be difficult enough to tell the judge in private; Jason has made it perfectly clear that the truth is not to be revealed. With Sandra sitting there—it makes him feel weak and uncomfortably warm. He wonders how he will describe what he has to describe without using vile language. Has Sandra heard these words? Has the judge?

The moral dilemma is that either he violates his client's trust and tells the truth, or respects the trust and lets the truth go untold and the client to the electric chair. That is the dilemma: not the typical hypothetical from a law-school ethics class, So-and-So overhearing something at a cocktail party at the country club, or noticing that an agreed-upon term is missing from the draft of a merger deal.

Either way, he loses. Either way, everyone looks to lose. He knows what will happen if he doesn't tell. If he does tell, Jason will certainly despise him. After all the work, all the struggle with the boy, that is a prospect he finds unbearable. Jason's death is also a prospect he finds unbearable. He feels, for an instant, as though he will never speak again—as though these two enormities simply negate him.

So it is with some surprise that he hears the words spilling from his lips, sketching the story of the McGuire men, finding proper but unmistakable words to describe what happened, what drove a seventeen year old to murder and mayhem.

By the time he's finished it's Sandra and the judge who are sitting there dumbstruck. No questions. No sound except the gentle ticktock of the grandfather clock in the corner, between two walls lined with *U.S.* Reports.

"Well," Bryan says, "that's the story."

Still nothing from Sandra, who looks as severe as ever

but rather paler. She knows what this means. She knows that the trial did not do justice, that the boy was acting, in effect, in self-defense, or at least under severe emotional duress. A number of ways of founding a defense on these revelations. She knows that, whatever the utility of the death penalty, the moral rightness of using it to punish truly atrocious crimes, she knows that Jason McGuire should not have been sentenced to die.

Still nothing.

"Mr. Delafield," the judge says at last, "that is certainly the most disturbing story I've heard in a long time, and you can believe that I will not sleep well tonight. I very much admire you and what you're trying to do against very great odds, and I admire your firm for giving you the latitude to operate in this case. But I cannot grant habeas corpus without some showing that the state proceedings have run afoul of the U.S. Constitution. It's just that simple, and we all know it. You haven't made such a showing.

"Your problem isn't the state, Counsel, it's your client. I can't urge you strongly enough to speak to him, persuade him to testify on his own behalf. His life is at stake, Counsel."

"I know that, Your Honor."

"Make sure he knows."

"I will, Your Honor."

There is no objection from Sandra.

Bryan is living, as he has been since March, in a little studio in a restored schoolhouse a few blocks from the capitol. He sees Caroline and Jessie often—several times a week, amicably. He's even slept with Caroline twice since he moved out.

It's a beautiful old building, just a few steps across a quiet park from the lake. The apartment itself is small and without personality but well-furnished with all the modern conveniences: an electric kitchen, new carpeting, space-age lights and an intercom. It's the first place Bryan's had by himself since he was in law school.

In his two-odd months of occupancy he has brought a good deal of clutter to the small space. There are no pictures on the walls, no photos or artwork, but the teak-veneer desk is loaded with manila folders, hornbooks, photocopied cases that might help Jason. A photo of Jason sits atop the desk, next to one of the three of them—Bryan, Jessie, Caroline. Wallet-size shots of Mort and Dawn.

I'll go back to them soon, he tells himself. When this thing is over. His mantra.

There's a twin bed, hidden in a sleeping alcove. The sheets are tangled and rumpled, and dirty clothes litter the floor. Dirty dishes in the sink, the garbage can filled with the tinfoil remains of TV dinners. All the markings of bachelorhood.

But the tired smell doesn't bother him, or the unsightliness, or the messages from Caroline on the answering machine, the note from Brett in the mailbox. All he is thinking about, as he comes through the door from a distracted afternoon, is what he knows he must do next.

He calls Caroline and leaves a message for her on their machine. *I'm going to Batavia tomorrow morning. Very important business. Don't worry. I'll let you know when I'm back in town.*

He does not want her to worry; knows that she will.

Bryan has never been to Batavia before but feels as though he knows it as well as he knows Monroe. It looks like a smaller version of the capital: the people look the same, sound the same; the buildings are made from the same red brick, gray fieldstone, white clapboard; the houses built in familiar prairie designs. A dusty drugstore on the corner of Main Street, selling Chiclets and chewing tobacco; a department store with mannequins in the windows, dowdy dresses, high-heeled pumps. The old railroad depot converted to a drive-up bank. All of it oddly comforting.

The Batavia County Courthouse is right in the middle of town, on a small square where a few elm trees grow. Everything is quiet and sleepy; even the flag in front of the courthouse barely moves. Bryan seems like a bolt of lightning as he jumps from his car and hurries up the broad steps, a leather case under his arm. The Audi draws some attention out here in Ford and Chevy land, but he is inside too quickly to notice.

First, file the motion for a stay of execution and a new trial immediately. Reason: new evidence. Also insist on seeing Judge Schulz. Explain the whole thing. Get him on your side. Persuade him that it's a fundamental question of justice.

He nearly bursts into tears as he enters the building and looks for directions. The judge isn't going to care. The judge is from this community: he knows what the murders meant to these people.

New trial! What the hell for? New evidence? Don't hand me that crap, Counsel. The kid confessed to the murders. Have you seen the police photos, Mr. Delafield? I believe we've got them on file somewhere. Ask the clerk. Take a little look-see. What more evidence do you need?

He doesn't cry. He looks at the directory and heads for the clerk's office on the second floor. Judge Schulz's chambers are just down the hall.

"I'm glad you could spare a few minutes."

"Well," says the judge, "it's not my usual practice, you know, but I know an urgent look when I see one."

"I'm here about Jason McGuire. You remember."

"Of course," says Judge Schulz. "You were here not so long ago looking for postconviction relief."

"Yes, that's right. I'm glad you remember."

"I'll never forget."

"Your Honor, let me get right to the point. I've just this minute filed with the clerk a motion for a stay of execution and a new trial for Jason. I've got a copy for you right here"—he hands over some papers—"so you can look it over."

"Counsel," Judge Schulz says, "forgive me for asking, but what the hell is this? What do you mean, new trial?"

Bryan hesitates. He has been moving in a dream, hoping, out of the corner of his eye, that Judge Schulz would somehow just sign the order and send him back to Monroe. Or at least read the motion and brief in support of it. But the dream is going dark.

"I know it's highly irregular," Bryan says, trying to suppress his rising anxiety. "Extremely. But, Judge, I don't know how to put this, some new evidence has recently come to light that will prove my client was acting in self-defense, or at least under extreme emotional duress."

"Self-defense?"

"That's right. Possibly."

"My God, man, they were asleep when he killed them! His father and brother! Self-defense? Don't insult me, Counsel."

"Your Honor, please," Bryan says. "Insulting you is the last thing I would ever do."

"I should hope so."

"Your Honor, there's really no way around this other than to tell you the story as I know it. My client does not want the story told, for reasons I'm sure you'll understand when I've finished telling you."

"I'm not getting any younger, Mr. Delafield."

Bryan tells, feeling somehow he is telling a ribald joke to a monk. Judge Schulz's face goes grim and unpleasant, and each word of the tale seems heavier than the last as Bryan forces them out one by one.

"Good Lord," says the judge. "Is that all?"

Bryan nods yes.

"I don't believe it. I knew Don McGuire. The boy's making it up to try to save his ass."

"He's not making it up. He doesn't want anyone to know. His trial lawyer never knew."

"So it would be his word on the stand."

"His mother and sister can give corroborating testimony."

The judge shakes his head. "I don't believe it."

"Judge," Bryan says, "if you could have seen what it took to get the story out of the kid, you'd know it's true. If he were making it up to clear himself, he would have told everyone. The papers, everyone."

"My God," the judge murmurs to himself. "Don McGuire."

"I can't explain it," Bryan says hurriedly. "All I know is that I've got a client nine days from execution who's got some talking to do."

For a long moment the judge stares out the window at the sky.

"Is he going to talk?" he asks at length. "I mean, he didn't say a word the first time, and that really amounts to a waiver. I can't see that I'm obligated to grant a new trial. Why didn't you bring this up in the postconviction proceeding?"

"Because, Your Honor, you know and I know that there was nothing wrong enough with the trial to get it thrown out. I mean, the confession thing still bothers me and I think that alone is grounds for reversal, but I've lost on that one every step of the way. I was hoping I could pull it off at some point, but I haven't been able to. The only way to straighten this whole thing out is with a new trial. It's the only way to do justice."

"You haven't answered my question," says Judge Schulz. "Is he willing to talk?"

Bryan hesitates a fatal instant. "I think so," he says, "yes. He will."

"Ah," says the judge, and there is another long pause. "You think he will."

"I know he will."

"You understand what these crimes did to this community."

"Yes."

"You understand how people around here feel about this young man."

"Yes."

"You know what they want."

"I know."

You know what *I* want, the judge thinks, and Bryan knows he is thinking it.

It's not your job to cave in to mob rule, but to see that justice is done, Bryan thinks and the judge knows.

Judge Schulz clasps his hands together and lays them on his desktop. He studies Bryan for a moment, moving his head slightly back and forth. No. I'm sorry, Counsel, I can't do it.

"All right," the judge says. "I'll stay the execution for a week pending disposition of this matter. But I'll give it to you straight, Mr. Delafield. I want to know the young man will testify to what you've told me today. I want him to tell me himself, and I want him to tell me that he's willing to testify to it in open court. Otherwise there's no point."

"I understand," Bryan says. "Shall I bring him here?"

"Too much bureaucratic razzmatazz," Judge Schulz says. "I'll speak to him at the prison. Tomorrow, 11 A.M. Don't look so stunned, Counsel. There's nothing to be gained by delay."

"I suppose not," says Bryan.

"I will expect to meet you in the warden's office at ten thirty," the judge says, somewhat formally. "You wish to be there, of course, when I meet with McGuire."

"Yes."

"Good."

"Ten thirty."

The judge nods in dismissal, and Bryan, after thanking him, hurries from the chambers.

20

Thirty days before, they move you to a special cell, near the green doors. They put a twenty-four hour watch on you, so you don't kill yourself before Gretchen can. There's a certain irony in the state's taking such elaborate precautions to ensure the safety of a condemned man as he heads down the final month toward the chair. Why not encourage them to hang themselves, or slit their wrists, or swallow an overdose of sleeping pills? That would be easier on everyone. The ritual is the real horror. Thinking about the time while everyone around you is quietly, grimly solicitous. But you have to be punished, and you have to know you're being punished, and why. So the condemned, in their last days, are taken care of like newborn infants. Every aspect of their lives is carefully monitored, controlled.

Jason has begun his last days.

They began quietly, when the warden came early on a Tuesday morning, before he was to go to the gym, to tell him the governor had signed the death warrant.

It's time, he said. This way.

So they led him to the special cell, next to the green doors, and two guards were always with him. No chatting, no abuse, no contact—just constant vigilance; quiet eyes, watchful. They were even watching when he jacked off late at night, when the rest of the row was sleeping. But they said nothing. Did nothing.

Perhaps there is nothing to say. He is not nervous, not worried; it's as though he's already dead and is just waiting for his body to take its 2,000 volts and stop working. Let's get it over with, he thinks, let's stop putting it off. Life is over and someone has forgotten to bag the lights.

Then he thinks of Bryan, of the face, the hands, the voice, and the tears come. He would like, at least, to see him one more time, to hear the voice, before they cook him. And then he feels cold and alone, and the guards are smoking their cigarettes, and sleep drifts in like fog.

There have been a few notes from Bryan. *Hang in there.* Or, *I'm working on it.* Or, *I'm seeing a judge this afternoon.* And his heart jumped a little. *I miss you. I'm going to try to see you as soon as I can.* His heart jumped a little more.

Then the warden came and led him to this cell. It's a matter of days now. They're starting to pick it up in the newspapers, on television. Grainy photographs of him all over; phone calls from reporters (he refuses them all).

It's not a bad cell as cells go. About the same size, with a bigger bed and a cleaner toilet bowl. The food is better, and they've taken to asking him what he would like. Steak? Shrimp? Fried chicken? He doesn't always get it, but things are definitely better. And bigger desserts.

Every day the chaplain comes to say prayers with him. At first he refused to go along, and the poor man stood there talking to himself like a crazy person. But after a few days

Jason let him into the cell, and they held hands while the chaplain read from the Bible about the Valley of Death and whispered to Jason not to worry.

God will bless you, he said. Don't be afraid.

I'm not afraid.

But he is.

I drive like a madman from Batavia back to Monroe even though there's no need. The stay will be faxed directly to the warden in Warrensville and confirmed by telephone. And there is time to breathe a little, anyway. We have dodged the electrode.

There is time, I tell myself, plenty of time. But I can't fight back the feeling that we're in the last two minutes of a football game, down four points, with the ball at our own ten and one time-out left. It can be done, yes, but don't bet your life on it.

When I get back to the apartment I strip off my clothes and get into the shower. The water runs over me for a long time, and the sound of the hot little drops beating on my back relaxes me for the first time in a long time. While I towel off I listen to the day's messages on the telephone.

Beep.

Hi, Bryan. Just wondering what you're up to. Call me when you get a chance.

Beep.

Hi. I got your message. I hope things went well. Call me when you can, maybe we can have dinner soon. I'll be home tonight. Call me. I miss you.

Beep.

Beep.

Also a note. *They've moved me into a special cell. The priest is here all the time, and I get good desserts. I guess*

they're serious. Are you ever coming here again? I under-
stand if you don't want to. I don't think I would if I was you.
Everyone says it smells really bad.

I put the note in a manila folder with all my other notes
from Jason. Then I pull on my underwear and an old
Brooks Brothers shirt and call Caroline.

"Hi," I say.

"You're back?"

"Fifteen minutes ago."

Her voice sounds odd, as though there's a crease in it.
Doubled over, in a way. I wonder if she's catching cold. Isn't
it almost June? It was a long hot drive back.

"How's Jessie?"

"She's OK. She asks about you all the time. She's making me bake all your favorite things. That mocha
cheesecake."

"You made that?"

"About fifteen minutes ago. Can I interest you?"

"Sure can," I say.

"In fact, there's a whole meal waiting," she says. "Your
favorite."

"Lemon chicken."

"With the cajun rice."

"Ohhh," I say. "I'll be right over."

"We'll be waiting."

And so they will.

After dinner Jessie goes off to the family room with
Dawn and Mort, both of whom seem to have grown
markedly in my absence. I help Caroline scrape the dishes
and get them ready for the dishwasher.

"She's so glad you're here," Caroline says. "She thinks
we hate each other."

"I'll talk to her before I go," I say. "Explain things."

"Maybe you can explain them to me, too," she says, and they might have been bitter words, but, bathed in tears, are not. "I don't hate *you*."

"Caroline," I say, "come on. What are you talking about?"

"I don't know," she says. "You're gone, I know that much."

"You're my wife," I say, slightly evading the issue. "You're the mother of our child."

"All I want to know is, when are you coming home? When is this stupid case ever going to be over?"

"I don't know," I murmur. "I don't know." That is not the real question. I know this; so does she. What I don't know is if and when and how we'll talk about it. And what we can possibly say.

"Do you want a divorce?" she blurts.

"I don't know," I say. "Maybe."

A long silence. The forks go in one basket, the spoons in another. She scrubs the dirty dishes industriously, so that it seems almost superfluous to load them into the machine. I note with some surprise that she even puts the Cuisinart work bowl into the dishwasher. I didn't know you could do that.

"Why?"

"The truth is," I say, "that I'm just not sure this is the kind of life I want to lead anymore."

"What do you mean, this kind of life?"

"I don't know," I admit. "The conventionality and everything. I'm not sure this is what I really want." I cannot quite believe I'm hearing this ode to bohemianism coming from my own mouth, but there it is.

"So what are you going to do, run off with your little murderer?" she says viciously. "Set up cell-keeping together?"

"No," I say forcefully. Important to maintain a keel of

reasonableness here. "You blame all our problems on him. Maybe he isn't the problem, did you ever think of that? Maybe he's just exposed it."

"I don't know what he's exposed, and I don't want to."

This embarrasses us both, and we redouble our clean-up efforts. But there isn't much left to do. I am reduced to returning the tub of margarine to the refrigerator. She takes out the garbage. When she returns I say:

"Caroline, I don't think we should talk about this anymore tonight. We're just going to get upset about nothing."

"I don't know about nothing."

"We'll talk about it soon. I'm going to speak to Jessie and then go home. I have to drive to Warrensville in the morning."

These words aren't meant to sting, but they do, and I can see a spasm of pain crossing her face. Before she has the chance to say something regrettable I hurry off to the family room.

"Your mother and I just need to be away from each other for a little while."

"Why?"

"Sometimes people need to be by themselves for a while. You've felt that way, haven't you?"

"No."

"The important thing," I say, "is that we both love you very much."

"When are you coming home?"

"I don't know, honey," I say, and I feel my heart crack a little. "Soon, I hope. But I don't know. Daddy's very busy right now."

"I need you to tell me stories at night," she says petulantly. "Mommy can't do the wolf."

"I'll come over real soon and tell you the wolf story," I say. "I promise. Right now Daddy's got to get going. He's got a busy day tomorrow."

I hug her and kiss her on the forehead and whisper that I love her, the whole while feeling like a complete shit.

At Brett's suggestion, we meet at White Knights. He's already there when I arrive, sitting alone at a table in his baggy, pegged khakis and Reeboks and white button-down. He is indistinguishable from the U. of C. under-graduates who are chattering at other tables.

"Hey."

"Hey."

"Want a beer? I'm buying."

"Fine."

He orders a pitcher and two glasses. Also some chips and salsa. He pours out the beer and we nibble at the chips.

"I actually have something I want to talk about tonight—for once," he says with a little laugh. "I'll bet you can guess what it is."

"Commercial paper."

"Eerie."

"I'm right."

"Pretty close," he says. "Collateral estoppel. Seriously. We've barely spoken to each other for months and I feel like it's my fault. I feel like ever since the last time we were here, you know, we haven't been on real good terms."

"I know."

"I want you to know that I regret what happened and that I apologize. I really do. I don't think either of us quite knew what we were doing." He takes a long slug of beer.

"What are you apologizing for?" I say. "I was there, too. I never tried to stop. I could have. It's not like I was bound and gagged. You want to know the truth?" I continue savagely. "It's all I think about at night."

"Me too."

"So," I say.

"More beer," he says, and orders another pitcher. We drink it, then another, talking about firm business and politics and college and the Supreme Court and the McGuire thing and on and on. The world grows warm and hazy and a little wobbly, and I'm happier than I can say that Brett is across the table, beautiful and alive. He pushes his leg up against mine and all I can think about is the warmth of it. Jason's hand was warm, too. At the thought I start to cry.

"You OK?"

"Fine," I say, lowering my head and reaching for my handkerchief. "I'm fine." But I can't stop crying. "I don't want him to die," I say. "I really don't."

Somehow we are out of White Knights and hurrying to Brett's car, which is parked in a ramp across the street. He hustles me into the back seat and climbs in alongside and takes me in his arms, murmuring. Gradually I cry myself out on his shoulder. But I don't let go, even after I stop.

"Is it true you left your wife?"

"I've got my own place, if that's what you mean."

"If I caused it," he says, "I'm sorry."

"It's more than that," I say. "You know."

He nods. We look at each other. Kiss deeply on the mouth. Extraordinary sensation. He breaks away suddenly and gets out of the back seat, into the driver's seat.

"There's a place we can go," he says. "It's close. I'll drive."

Too woozy to argue.

*   *   *

The place is called The Cellar. It's in the basement of an old hotel not six blocks from my studio. The front of the hotel is a fancy restaurant where I've eaten many a lunch. (At least two with Brett.) We go to the back, through an unmarked door, down some concrete stairs into a bar that seems like a cross between a cave and the Starship *Enterprise*. Long dark corridors, crowding darkness. Flashing lights of many colors. We work our way through the mob, which I am not surprised to notice is all male. Jeans, T-shirts, mustaches, leather.

A back room. A large video screen on the far wall. Dozens of sets of eyes fixed on the images of naked blonde boys as they cavort in a mountain park. They are doing something nasty on the hood of a Jeep convertible. We see it in slow motion, from several angles. I immediately get an erection. Brett is brushing against me; we lean against the wall and he casually drapes an arm around my shoulder.

"I come here sometimes," he says, "when I really need to. It clears my mind."

I nod.

We watch some more blond boys. I glance down at Brett and notice that he is cradling himself. He notices I'm noticing and smiles. I brush a hand there, feel the bulge in his khakis. His hand on me.

"Vámonos."

"Yes."

"Your place. My roommate . . ."

"Yes."

And though I am still quite drunk, I am also lucid enough to be thinking that he reminds me of Jason. Hornier. Sadder. We go.

21

Jason is taking a nap, maybe dreaming, fists curled, legs drawn into the fetal position, when Bryan arrives at the prison's main gate at about nine thirty. An hour before the judge; plenty of time to meet with Jason, apprise him of the situation. There is some confusion among the guards, who sense his high anxiety and are suspicious of it, but after a phone call from the guardhouse to the warden's office Bryan is waved through.

Warden Riley is sitting at his old green metal desk filling out papers. His office looks like Frank Furillo's, smells strongly of cigarette smoke. The secretary, a dumpy gray grouchy woman of vague middle age, tells Bryan, "Go in," and he does.

"Ah, well, Counselor, good to see you again," Riley says. "I'm sorry about the delay down at the gate. You'd think those guys'd know you by sight by now." He looks up and smiles without any hint of warmth.

"Warden, let me tell you why I'm here. My client has received a stay of execution—"

"Yes," says the warden, lighting up an unfiltered Camel. He waves a sheet of paper. "Fax came in yesterday afternoon. Right before dinner. Wonderful news. Spoke to the judge yesterday afternoon. He must be about halfway here by now."

"—in order to give me a chance to uncover evidence that may lead to a new trial."

"Well, we wouldn't want to do an injustice to these murderers, would we, Counsel? We want to give them every chance to wriggle off the hook. Thank goodness for you lawyers."

Pause.

"I suppose you'll be wanting to see him now," the warden continues with a tired grunt. "One of the boys'll take you up. The conference room is open most of the day today, I believe."

"I wonder if we might use one of the trailers."

"You really do have balls, don't you, Mr. Delafield," Riley says, and laughs a laugh of genuine pleasure. "Well, 'course it was you and your kind got the boy here in the first place. But he ain't going to be around much longer—with all due respect—and I don't see the point of denying him this or that. Sure, if he wants to go with you."

"Thank you."

"Think nothing of it."

A guard takes him through two sets of steel doors, down a long corridor, right, left, through two more sets of steel doors, right again and onto death row. Listless men in small cells, like mice in a laboratory; they smoke, read, stare. There are the green doors. There's the special cell where they've moved Jason. He's lounging in his underwear wiping sleep from his eyes as Bryan comes up. Bryan turns away, gives the boy a minute to collect himself, cover his vulnerability. But Bryan calls out.

"Hey, man," he says. "God, what are you doing here?"

Bryan is still staring at the doors. Bolted shut, laced with rivets, like the bulkhead of a submarine. The voice touches him, brings him back.

"Terrific news," he says. "I got a stay. We got a stay. *You* got a stay, I mean. For at least a week."

A week.

He hands Jason a copy of Judge Schulz's order.

"This is the same bastard who sentenced me," Jason says calmly. "He change his mind or something?"

"We have to talk about that," Bryan says. "I've arranged for us to have some time in one of the trailers. Where we spent that weekend. You remember."

"Yeah," Jason said. "Sure."

"Meantime you get out of this cell."

There is an element of joy here, as between two brothers who haven't seen each other in months meeting at their hometown airport on Christmas Eve. Embracing in a light snowfall, climbing into their parents' Ford for the ride home. Timeless sentimentality. But "stay of execution" is a phrase Bryan cannot speak in full in front of Jason. And the green doors are still there, and even Bryan has heard of what lies beyond them.

It isn't Christmas Eve.

A different trailer, but the same moldy smell, guards hovering around outside. Bryan sits down at the table and pulls another copy of Judge Schulz's order from his briefcase. Jason wanders from window to window gazing out on the prison landscape. Spring makes even this place less grim for a time: the leaves are budding on the trees, and brightly colored wildflowers have sprung up in the mud. On the other side of the prison buildings, tax cheats and perjurers are out toiling in the fields of the prison farm. Potatoes, green peppers, broccoli, squash, corn. A good part of the produce they grow is used by the prison commissary; the rest is given to charities in Warrensville and Monroe. The corn goes to the pigs. From their fields the petty crooks can look up to the second-floor windows that surround the windowless room where Gretchen waits.

"Well," Bryan says, "we finally caught a break." He shuffles through the order; Jason sits in a dilapidated easy chair.

"Yeah." He gets up and starts to move around again. "I want to thank you, man, for everything you've done for me. You're a great lawyer. I'm sorry I'm such an asshole."

"Don't thank me yet," Bryan says. "We're just getting started."

"Yeah."

"Listen," Bryan says, "let me give you the complete lowdown." Reluctantly Jason looks his way. "Hey," Bryan says. "We can do this thing. We can pull it off."

"Hit me."

"Judge Schulz has agreed to grant you a new trial. I spoke with him about it yesterday."

"What's the point of a new trial?"

"Are you kidding? If we don't get you off completely, we'll at least get it down to manslaughter or second-degree murder."

"How?"

"By showing," Bryan says, "that this wasn't an unprovoked attack. That you had a reason for what you did. That you were acting in self-defense, possibly."

"You mean about my dad and brother and everything."

"Yes."

Jason looks out the window again, pulls at his left thumb. "We've been over this," he says. "I'm not going to talk about it."

"Look," Bryan says gently. "It's not going to be that difficult. All you have to do is confirm the story to the judge, agree to be cross-examined about it in court. We'll let the state read your testimony in written form—tell them it's too traumatic to talk about from square one." He reaches into his briefcase and pulls out a sheaf of papers with single-space typing on it. "The judge'll be here in less than an hour. He wants to hear straight from your lips that you'll do it. Here. I wrote this up. Read it over and tell me if it's accurate."

Jason takes the papers and starts to read. Bryan watches his face closely, but the boy shows no signs of emotion.

"The judge is coming here?"

"Yes."

"To see me?"

"Yes."

"'And further,'" he reads out loud, "'I acknowledge that I will submit to cross-examination on these issues at retrial.' What does that mean?"

"It means," Bryan says carefully, "that the other side can ask you questions about this stuff."

"I told you I can't talk about it."

Bryan gets up and grabs him by the shoulders. "Stop giving me that crap," he says. "You've got to."

Jason shakes his head violently. "I won't," he says, and starts to cry. "I won't." And Bryan is crying too, pulling away from him.

"Think about what you're saying," Bryan says. "That you'd rather die than tell the truth. That you'd rather let the state kill you than to let the world know that you're not some crazy, evil kid. You had a reason, dammit. Let them know."

"Let them know I'm a queer," Jason says through soft, bitter sobs. "Let them know. Should I tell them what I was doing half the time? That I liked it?"

"You were abused, don't you see?" Bryan says. "Physical assault. They were violating your body. Doesn't make any difference if you thought you liked it or not. What you thought at all. What you did."

"Fuck," Jason says, a little less hysterically now. "I'm not a queer."

"I'll tell you something," Bryan says. "A year ago I would have said, 'Fine. You want to get fried in that chair, that's your problem. You don't want to tell the truth to save your own skin, I'll live with it. Not me who's going to get roasted.' But I don't feel that way any more," he continues, voice rising. "I care about you. I want justice, I want you out of here. I can't bear the thought—"

He breaks off, mistrusting his voice, feelings: what is he saying? Has Caroline been right all along? What kind of lawyer is he, making these emotional statements to clients? *Can't bear the thought?*

"I don't want to die," Jason says in a whisper.

"Then don't."

Four guards lead Jason into a special conference room just off the warden's office. It's a more comfortable room than the other, with well-worn leather chairs and a dark oak table. The smells of coffee and cigarette smoke mingle.

The judge and Bryan are already waiting there, talking softly between themselves. For a moment it's as though they are unaware of Jason's arrival. He stands there awkwardly in his shackles, the guards silent beside him.

"Jason," Judge Schulz says firmly, smoothly, "please sit down." He motions to the guards to wait outside, and they withdraw. Jason remains in his shackles. "Let's get right to the point," the judge continues. "As I'm sure you know, Mr. Delafield and I had quite a conversation yesterday at my chambers in Batavia. He explained to me some key facts about your case that were not disclosed at trial. Facts that, I must say, if true, rather change the shape of things."

Jason's expression is flat, but he fidgets. Bryan nods encouragement, like a father whose son is being bawled out by the school principal for throwing snowballs at the girls.

"Without going into excruciating detail," the judge says, with some distaste, "which I daresay isn't necessary, I would like to talk to you briefly about this matter so that I know I've got it straight in my mind. I would also like us to agree on how to proceed."

"The new trial," Bryan says.

"I am in fact prepared to grant you a new trial," Judge Schulz says, "on a few conditions we will discuss in a moment. But first I would like to get the substance of the matter out of the way. Mr. Delafield has told me that your father and brother took sexual liberties with you. Repeatedly and over a period of many months. Is this true?"

Jason looks helplessly at Bryan, who nods again. He nods faintly. The judge sighs.

"It is not up to me to judge whether you are telling the truth about this," he says gravely, "although I am inclined to believe you are. In the end it will be for the jury to decide. But there has been some question whether you are willing to talk about the matter at all in court. Mr. Delafield tells me he has shown you the written statement he is prepared to submit on your behalf, setting out the details of this matter. This will spare you the need to tell the entire story from the beginning.

"But," the judge continues, "I need your assurance that you will allow yourself to be cross-examined on the issue by the state."

"That you will answer the prosecutor's questions," Bryan says.

"I know it is a painful business for you," says Judge Schulz. "It is for all of us. But the evidence cannot be admitted without giving the state the chance to question you about it. And without the new evidence, there's no point in a new trial."

Bryan is nodding again, hoping to get Jason to go along as before. But the boy remains silent, motionless.

"Will you agree to sign the statement and be cross-examined about it at a new trial?" the judge asks. "That's what I need to know."

Bryan nods yes. Jason looks at him with an expression of weary resignation. All right, all right, he says with his body, and Bryan feels a shiver of elation. He agrees. There will be a new trial, conviction on a lesser count, a moderate sentence. All will be well.

"No."

"I'm sorry," says the judge, confused. "Mr. Delafield, I thought we had everything ironed out."

"So did I, Your Honor. Jason, what do you mean, no? You told me you'd do it."

Silence.

"You understand what's at stake, young man," the judge says. "Your testimony is crucial. Indispensable. If you aren't willing to give it, there's no point in a new trial."

"I'm sorry, Judge," Jason says. "I just can't."

"Your Honor," Bryan says desperately, "perhaps if I conferred again with my client—"

"Counsel, you have had more than enough time to confer with your client. He is unwilling to cooperate."

"Please!"

The judge gives him a skeptical stare. "I'll wait another hour," he says at length. "That's all. This is turning into a wild-goose chase. I have other business to attend to."

"I understand, Your Honor," Bryan says. "We'll be back in less time than that." And, guards in tow, he hurries Jason out of the conference room and the building, across the prison grounds, and back to the trailer.

". . . last night," Bryan is saying.

After a long pause. Jason still wandering from window to window. The guard burst in a while ago, found them speechless, left talking to himself.

"Yeah?"

Bryan feels an odd mix of exhilaration and shame well up inside him.

"I met someone," he says. "From work. About 25. Looks a lot like you. We went to my place."

"So you are queer," Jason says in a voice devoid of judgment. "I knew it."

"You know what I did this morning?"

"Got an AIDS test."

"I came here. I spoke to the warden. I met with Judge Schulz. I arranged this meeting in this trailer."

"So? I hate these fuckin' trailers. They smell like shit, like fuckin' murderers." Cough.

"The point," Bryan says slowly, "is that I'm here doing my job. Tomorrow I'll be doing my job and seeing my daughter and dealing with my wife. I'll be living my life.

Maybe I'll see this prison again, maybe not. But either way, I'll survive."

"You're a lawyer," Jason says. "They're not fuckin' going to pick on you. You went to school. You got money. What do I got?"

"You've got me."

"What good is that?" No malice in the voice; only sadness.

"I'll tell you what good it is. It means I'll always be there for you. It means I care about you, that I'll help you any way I can. I mean it."

"Aw, man," Jason says, and Bryan tries in vain to read the meaning of the smooth stony syllables.

"I don't know what to say," Bryan says. It's been almost an hour; he is exhausted, slumped in the same chair. Papers still scattered on the table in front of him.

"Don't say anything," Jason says, and comes up behind him. Bryan feels the boy's hands on his neck, warm and strong: a sudden pulse of fear. This is what happens in prisons. Unaccountable murders. No one talks about them; no one is ever charged. No one cares. Vermin killing vermin. Lift rug and sweep. That's why these people are here in the first place. They kill for no reason, without warning. Quickly and efficiently.

But the hands knead and massage, running up the back of his head, through his hair; fingers rubbing gently behind his ears, down his shoulders, circling, pulling, rubbing. Tension ebbs; the mind becomes lucid.

"I don't get it," Bryan says.

"Please let's not talk about it anymore." The hands range down Bryan's back, along his arms; his fingers stretch involuntarily.

"I just don't get it."

"Feel good?"

A murmur of pleasure.

"Does your friend do this for you?"

"What friend?"

"Your friend from last night."

"We're not an item," Bryan says, "if that's what you mean."

"Whatever. Does he do this for you?"

"No."

"Are you going to live with him?"

"No."

"Why not?"

"Because I don't love him."

"Oh."

Jason pulls out Bryan's shirttails and pushes him forward onto the table so he can work on his bare back.

"You feel tense," he says.

"I suppose you don't."

"No," he says, "not really."

"The guard," Bryan says weakly.

"Don't worry." He rubs some more. "Why don't you love him?"

"Brett?"

"You never told me his name."

"Just don't."

"Are you in love with anyone?"

"I don't know."

"What happens if I tell him I'll talk?"

Another surge of hope. "If you sign the statement and agree to be cross-examined," Bryan says, "you'll get a new trial. That's for sure. I can't guarantee what will happen, but I know you won't be convicted of capital murder. It'd either be second-degree murder or manslaughter. Probably manslaughter. I don't know—five years, maybe. Paroled for good behavior in two." Hard not to babble; talk up the good news and it comes true. That's the way it's done nowadays. Like politics.

"I mean after that."

"What do you mean, after that?"

"I mean after I get out."

"You've thought further ahead than I have," Bryan says. "I'm not looking much past the new trial."

"I mean, will I ever see you again? Will you be there for me like you say you will?"

"You know I will."

"Do you love me?"

Bryan picks his head up from the table and turns to look at Jason. The word gives him another pinch of fright. Sharper than the touch of hands.

"I love you," Jason says. "I always wanted to tell you. I always wanted you to know. Now you know." And, although he is still standing, he puts his arms around Bryan from behind and rests his head against Bryan's neck.

"I deserve to die," he whispers in Bryan's ear.

In the Supreme Court
of the United States

McGuire v. Riley, Warden.
No. CR-6897
Order

July 7. The application for stay of execution of the sentence of death, presented to Justice Washington and by her referred to the Court, is denied. The petition for certiorari is denied.

Dissenting statement by Justices Becker, Howard, and Washington.

22

I look at my watch and it's almost midnight. Exhausted but not tired: coffee jumping through me. Five, maybe six cups. All I can think about is getting out of here, getting into the car, going back. The reporters around me are restless, wondering if there's going to be a delay, how long they're going to be stuck out here.

Jason and I played chess for several hours after dinner in the special cell where they keep them just before. He got his own cell back for a few weeks, but the stay expired and the governor signed another warrant. The plea for clemency failed, as I knew it would. The governor is facing a difficult reelection battle in the fall, and he cannot afford to be perceived as soft on criminals.

"I'm sorry," he told me, sitting between his flags. "It is simply not appropriate for me to interfere with the judgment of our courts in this case."

"But Governor," I said, "clearly the boy was convicted and sentenced by a jury that didn't have the most crucial fact of all before it."

"I am truly sorry, Mr. Delafield," the governor said. "Do you know what it would mean if I granted clemency to Jason McGuire? Can you imagine the uproar?"

Plus, I thought, you'd get about three votes in November.

"Thank you," I said formally and stalked out. Numb.

Dinner: deep-fried shrimp, french fries, a Caesar salad, Coke, chocolate chocolate-chip ice cream. I had a cheeseburger and a Diet 7-Up. Nausea churns.

He's gotten much better at chess. I used to be able to mate him in seven or eight moves, but tonight we played to two stalemates before the guards came in at eleven and told me I had to leave. The priest was coming.

I don't want to see the goddamn priest, he said, but the man was already waiting outside.

"A moment alone?" I asked the guards. They looked at each other, then nodded and backed out of the cell, more or less out of earshot. I turned to Jason and felt my eyes growing hot. One by one he knocked all the chess pieces over.

"I guess this is it," he said. "Thanks for everything you've done for me. I know it must have seemed like I didn't care half the time, but I really did."

"I tried," I said, my voice cracking. "I really did. I feel like I've let you down."

He smiled and shook his head.

"No way, man."

Somehow I moved over to him and took him in my arms and held back the tears. He held me, too. The first time we ever embraced. I ran my hand over his neck, smooth and strong; over his head, now shorn of its hair. His scalp felt hard, invulnerable.

"I'll never understand this," I said.

"Me neither."

We looked at each other, and I held his face in my hands; I looked into those clear green eyes, cat's eyes, and gently brushed my lips across his. I didn't care if the priest could see, if the guards could see. I didn't care if they burst out laughing, or hit me with their rifle butts. I didn't care. Shoot me dead.

"I'll always think of you," I said. "I'll never forget."

"Me neither."

Hard to let go. At length there was a discreet rattling of keys in the lock, and one of the guards said, "I'm afraid your time's up, Mr. Delafield."

Mr. Delafield.

"Goodbye," I said.

"Goodbye," he said with a sigh, and sat back down at the little pine table to rearrange the chess pieces. There might be time for one more game with the priest. He did not look at me as I was escorted out of the holding cell and toward the witness box. Let's go, kid, I could hear them saying, It's time.

The black curtains part. A door opens on the right, and four guards lead Jason into the small chamber with its horrible green paint. He does not glance toward the witness box—toward me or the reporters, who are alert now, pencils poised, to record all the details, the timing, the final statement, all the rest, for the newswires. They are going to get their story after all.

The warden reads the death warrant. *Whereas, Jason Lee McGuire was found guilty of capital murder and sentenced to death....*

Jason is calm. He sits down in the chair, sits calmly while they fasten the leather straps around his legs, wrists, chest, chin. He stares straight ahead while they roll up his left pant leg to attach one electrode. He holds his head stiffly while they attach the other to his skull. His hands clutch the arms of the chair, as though he's about to ride a roller coaster.

It is therefore ordered that the sentence of death be executed upon Jason Lee McGuire. . . .

The guards retreat.

In testimony whereof, I have hereunto set my hand. . . . The warden intones the governor's name, hands the document to an aide. He comes forward and speaks to Jason. Do you have anything you would like to say?

No sir.

It is now six minutes past midnight. A guard approaches Jason one last time, to place the black hood over his head. Just before it falls he catches my eye, and we exchange a long steady stare that seems to say more than the words we exchanged ever did. The black cloth falls, and the guard steps away.

The warden nods twice, almost imperceptibly, toward a window behind the chair, where a man in a black robe and a hood stands over a control board. He flips a toggle switch: 2,200 volts.

Jason jumps against the straps, the veins in his forearms bulging, his hands clawing at the arms of the chair. The skin of his forearms—the only bit of his flesh I can still see—turns bright red, and steam rises. Or smoke? There is a horrible, sweet-acrid smell, a faint sizzling sound, and I struggle not to throw up in front of my fellow witnesses. After some seconds, Jason slumps to his left, and his hands slowly unclench.

Mine do not.